A note from the editor...

Well, this is it—the last m
We've had a good run, bu
things have to end someti
Temptation is very, *very* go

When we celebrated our twentieth anniversary last year, we personified the series as a twenty-year-old woman. She was young, legal (well, almost) and old enough to get into trouble. Well, now that she's twenty-one and officially legal, she's leaving home. And she's going to be missed.

I'd like to take this opportunity to thank the countless number of authors who have given me, and other Harlequin Temptation editors past and present, so many hours of enjoyable reading. They made working at Harlequin an absolute pleasure.

I'd also like to thank our loyal readers for all their support over the past twenty-one years. Never forget—you are the reason we all do what we do. (Check out the back autograph section if you don't believe me.)

But this doesn't have to be the end....

Next month Harlequin Blaze increases to six books, and will be bringing the best of Harlequin Temptation along with it. Look for more books in THE WRONG BED, 24 HOURS and THE MIGHTY QUINNS miniseries. And don't miss Blazing new stories by your favorite Temptation authors. Drop in at tryblaze.com for details.

It's going to be a lot of fun. I hope you can join us.

Brenda Chin
Associate Senior Editor
Temptation/Blaze

"I'm tired of being cautious and shy."

Laine looked at him. "I took this job with the magazine for the pay raise, but it's also part of my journey to be more assertive and confident."

The tension dispelled, Steve kissed her palm. "How assertive are we talking about?"

She lifted herself out of her seat, hiked her dress up, then swung her leg over his lap and straddled him.

"That's pretty assertive."

Laine grinned. "When you want something..." She traced his bottom lip with her finger. "Or someone..."

Eyes wide, he slid his hands up her sides. "I don't want our first time to be in a car," he said without much conviction.

Leaning down, she tongued his earlobe. "Sometimes assertiveness is all about the timing." She pressed her hips against his. "And this isn't our first time."

WENDY ETHERINGTON

THE ELEVENTH HOUR

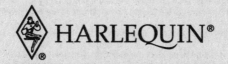

HARLEQUIN®

TORONTO • NEW YORK • LONDON
AMSTERDAM • PARIS • SYDNEY • HAMBURG
STOCKHOLM • ATHENS • TOKYO • MILAN • MADRID
PRAGUE • WARSAW • BUDAPEST • AUCKLAND

ISBN 0-373-69227-7

THE ELEVENTH HOUR

Copyright © 2005 by Etherington, Inc.

www.eHarlequin.com

Printed in U.S.A.

Dear Reader,

Things always seem to come full circle, don't they?

I started these stories about the Kimball family with the concept of heroes and their importance in both life and fiction very much on my mind. I was writing the first one in September 2001 and now here we are years later with the definition of an "American Hero" changed and intensified forever.

In the lives of the Kimballs it's finally "Baby" Steven's turn. Hopefully he will measure up to your personal definition of a hero as he finds himself and the love of his life.

While my story comes full circle, so does Harlequin Temptation. After twenty years of love, drama and laughter, this month marks the end of the line in North America. I hope the books have been as pleasurable for you to read as they have been for us authors to write.

Drop me a line anytime via my Web site, www.wendyetherington.com, or by regular mail at P.O. Box 3016, Irmo, SC 29063.

Take care and happy reading!

Wendy Etherington

Books by Wendy Etherington

HARLEQUIN TEMPTATION
944—PRIVATE LIES
958—ARE YOU LONESOME TONIGHT?
998—SPARKING HIS INTEREST

HARLEQUIN FLIPSIDE
29—IF THE STILETTO FITS...

This book is dedicated in memory
of Robert "Scooter" Haines, a great American hero
to both his country and his family.

Prologue

WITH A HOLLOW STOMACH, Laine Sheehan sank onto a bar stool. She rested her elbows on the glossy mahogany bar that had been in her family for so long, still stunned by the news.

"It's over," her sister, Cat, announced as she tossed ice into a cocktail shaker. "I knew those biddies from the historical society would reject us. The city wants a new road, so we're out."

Laine realized her sister's bravado was a front; this was killing her.

Temptation would soon be no more.

As her and Cat's two closest friends, Gracie and Tess, flanked her and launched commiserations at her sister, Laine clutched the envelope the leader of the historical society had given her as they'd walked out of the courtroom earlier.

She reread the enclosed letter, the knot of disappointment that had formed in her stomach tightening to anger.

Thank you for applying to the Kendall, Texas, Historical Society...your establishment, Temptation, while having been in your family for more than

*twenty years, unfortunately doesn't qualify for reg-
istry in our society…send our best wishes…*

"Blah, blah, blah," she said under her breath.

Laine had never considered failure. She'd planned
an attack and executed it. The city wouldn't be asi-
nine enough to throw out two thriving businesses—
Temptation and Gracie's bookstore next door—for a
wider stretch of asphalt. It wasn't right. Or fair.

Okay, maybe they hadn't been thriving lately, but
that was only because the city's big road project had
already caused lane closures, detours and had cut
into the building's parking. When the work was
done, their customers would come back.

Gracie sighed. "Where am I going to store all those
books if I can't find a new place in thirty days?"

"I'll never find another job as good as this one,"
Tess said.

"How are we going to explain this to Mom?"
Laine asked Cat.

Tess patted her hand. "Brenda will understand.
She'll be pissed, but she'll deal with it."

Laine could feel angry tears clogging her throat.
She wrapped her hand around the stem of her martini glass and had to resist the urge to hurl it across
the room. "I just can't believe it."

Cat raised an eyebrow. "Had faith in the system,
Lainey dear?"

Glaring at her sister for both the hated nickname
and her caustic attitude, Laine crushed the letter in
her fist. Of all the times she'd pulled Cat—kicking
and screaming—out of one fix or another, she

couldn't believe she hadn't succeeded this time. "Yes, I did. This isn't right. How can they just take away everything we've worked for?"

Looking miserable, Gracie sipped her drink. "Because they can."

Laine dropped the crumpled letter and envelope onto the bar, then shoved back her stool and turned away. They'd failed. *She'd* failed.

Though the idea to approach the historical society had been Gracie's, Laine had taken charge of the process—compiling Gracie's research, filing the paperwork, calling frequently for updates. As always, she'd handled everything down to the tiniest detail and she was the one who'd convinced the others that with the right plan, the right argument, there was hope they could convince the city not to demolish their building.

And if she was feeling this lousy, she couldn't imagine her sister's emotional turmoil. The bar was her baby. Though Laine balanced the books, made the work schedules, booked local bands for the weekends, ordered supplies and occasionally played barmaid, Cat worked daily and nightly behind that long mahogany bar. Temptation was her job and her life.

While Laine kept herself, her family and everybody else on schedule and organized, Cat relied on little but her guts and wits.

Which was why now—more than ever—Laine had to take up the slack.

Unlike Cat, she had a career outside the bar, one that would hopefully save them financially. After years as a photographer for a lifestyle magazine, she'd been hired recently at *Century*, a national, hard-hitting news publication. The assignments were pushing her past the comfort zone she'd fallen into, but for the raise she was getting, she'd find a way to manage. Her paycheck had just become essential. She couldn't imagine Cat surviving on her own, and Laine couldn't let her sister down.

Gracie appeared next to her, putting her arm around Laine's waist. "This isn't your fault."

Laine shared a strained smile with her friend. "Sure it is. If I'd talked to the right person, made the right argument…"

"The city would still be steamrolling over our businesses."

"Maybe." Avoiding the subject of the bar closing, Laine glanced at her longtime friend. Gracie had grown up with her and Cat, then Tess had come along a few years later looking for a short-term job and had never left. The four of them had been through a lot together and had always found time for weekly poker at table seven. "What are you going to do now?"

"Find a new place for the bookstore, I guess," Gracie said with a shrug. "I owe it to Aunt Fran."

"I've got money from my new job." Which she really wasn't in a position to offer, but the bookstore was also Gracie's only means of income. "If you need anything—"

"I'll be fine. You shouldn't take on so much. There's nothing more you can do here. Why don't you go away for a few days. Take some time for yourself."

Laine shook her head. "I can't. I've only done a few assignments for the magazine. Not to mention

Aunt Jen is making me crazy. Those wildfires in California are threatening—"

Well, damn. Aunt Jen was relying on her, too. Even in the path of a forest fire, Jen had vowed never to leave her precious, hundred-year-old home.

Laine felt as if she was being pulled in a dozen different directions.

Money. The bar. Her job. Aunt Jen. The wildfire.

And she suddenly realized the only way to make it all work was to combine everything. If she could convince her editor to let her do a pictorial on the wildfire, she could earn a living and make sure stubborn Aunt Jen evacuated when necessary.

Cat wouldn't be happy if she left, but neither could she deny that the income was vital. Her sister would just have to prepare the bar for closing and hold down the fort until she got back.

She glanced over her shoulder at Cat, who was mumbling something to Tess and looking miserable.

Maybe the responsibility would be good for her sister. Maybe the time by herself would urge her to finally get her life together. "June thirtieth, right?" she asked Gracie.

"That's D-day apparently. Less than three weeks."

Would her editor go for her assignment suggestion? There was only one way to find out.

1

"So, how about me in California?" Laine asked, rocking forward on her toes as she stood in front of her boss's imposingly disorganized desk.

Mac Solomon's silver-and-black eyebrows drew together. "That's a big assignment."

"I'm ready." *Or in desperate financial straits—take your pick.*

"Maybe. You know my philosophy, right? Bad news sells better than good."

"I remember." And she knew how the assignment game was played with her boss—the aggressive, pushy photographer always won. Even if, deep down, she was scared to death of getting within ten miles of a raging wildfire. "You'll be pleased to hear they've called in an arson investigator."

"I want something on this dead smoke jumper."

Laine swallowed and avoided glancing at the Internet story and picture she'd laid on her boss's desk. Tommy Robbins had died five days ago fighting the northern California wildfire. In what seemed like a lifetime ago, she'd known him. He'd been a close friend of a guy she'd dated the summer she'd lived with Aunt Jen after her college graduation.

Those carefree days seven years ago had ended in heartbreak, and now her trip back would begin there. Part of her dreaded going. The rest of her relished the challenge.

"I'll get you all you want on smoke jumping," she said.

Her former lover, Steve Kimball, might not be thrilled to see her, but his ego certainly wouldn't deny her the opportunity to follow him around and take pictures of him doing heroic stuff. Of course, she'd have to fight off the gaggle of women surrounding him, but that shouldn't feel like a kick in the teeth this time around.

Mac harrumphed. "I want some action shots. Destruction and flames."

"This story is not just about the fire itself, you know. The reports are that the blaze could consume most of the town of Fairfax. There will be evacuations, acts of courage, a community pulling together. It could be a real uplifting piece."

"Tears are always good sellers."

"Ah, Mac, you're all heart."

"I'm all business, Laine. You know that. We have that in common."

While she considered herself a professional, she certainly hoped she never reached the jaded bad-news-sells-better-than-good status that Mac had.

"You'll get the best," she said.

"I want daily updates. E-mail me what you've got. If you can come up with a real action shot, maybe we'll talk about the cover."

A big fat bonus came with the cover shot. That

would come in handy. Maybe she could pull together enough funds to send Cat back to school, as she'd once dreamed of doing.

"Not too much sissified human-interest crap," Mac went on.

Since feel-good, human-interest pictures had always been her specialty, Laine had to swallow that blow to her pride. "I'll try to restrain myself."

"I should be sending one of my guys to cover this, not the new girl."

Nothing like the added pressure of having a sexist for an editor. "But they don't have a connection with the smoke jumpers. Or an in with the chief in charge of the operation. I do."

Thank you, Aunt Jen. Provided Laine cleared her shoots with him and supplied the forestry service with copies of her photos for training purposes, the chief had agreed to sign releases for the magazine and get her close to the fire.

"Hmmph."

"I know the people in this town, remember? They're a close-knit group. They're not going to let just anybody wander around taking their picture."

Of course, close to the people and close to the fire were two entirely different propositions, but Laine had little choice. She'd taken this job not just for money, but for new challenges. She'd decided she couldn't bear photographing yet another rose show or "garden of the month," such as the layouts she'd done for *Texas Living*. It was time she proved to Mac—and herself—that she was ready for a new test in her career.

"I'm the best person for this assignment," she added.

"Yeah, sure." Mac shuffled through the papers scattered across his desk. "Then what are ya standin' here for?"

STEVE KIMBALL SHIFTED the heavy supply pack onto his shoulder as he climbed into the forestry service transport truck. He'd spent two exhausting days digging a fire line, cutting down trees and clearing brush, trying to deprive the raging flames of fuel. He was dirty, frustrated and exhausted. The men around him didn't look much better. Faces black with soot, eyes downcast and solemn.

Though it had been a long time since he'd been part of a smoke jumper team, he knew they were usually energized by the flight, parachuting through the heat and smoke-choked sky, the feeling that they were making progress blocking the spread of a fire that couldn't be fought in ordinary ways.

But the cockiness and exhilaration hadn't come for Steve. He supposed he shouldn't have expected it. He was in the last place he wanted to be, for the worst reason in the world.

He'd buried one of his closest friends a week ago. The crew he was now part of had lost one of their best.

"Well, this sucks," Josh Burke commented as he slumped on the bench seat and laid his head back against the dark green canvas surrounding the truck bed.

Of course, he wasn't just talking about the wildfire. Almost five thousand acres of beautiful northern California forestland had burned so far, with the flames creeping closer to civilization by the hour. If they didn't get some rain soon, they would have to start evacuating the small community of Fairfax, the town where Josh grew up and Steve had lived during the three years he'd been a full-time smoke jumper. If the fire got beyond that, there was nothing standing between the blaze and the more densely populated city of Redding.

No one mentioned these dire details, or the late Tommy Robbins. They were men after all. Smoke jumpers. Firefighters. Heroes.

Yeah, right.

"Let's send Kimball into town for women," Cole Taylor said.

"You don't buy them at the store," Steve said, bracing himself as the truck bounced along the country highway. Besides, he didn't want company. He just wanted the meal that awaited them at base camp, then to collapse on the guest bed in Josh's apartment.

Josh raised his head long enough to glance at Steve. "We'd have to clean him up first. Not even Mr. Magic could get a woman looking like that."

"Mr. Magic?" one of the younger guys asked.

Josh lay back again, casually folding his hands across his stomach. "Women love him. Go figure. Personally, I don't see it."

Steve forced himself to smile, relieved to have something to focus on besides death and flames. He could grieve and feel sorry for himself when he was alone later. Right now he had a role to fill—the fun guy, the one who couldn't wait to charge the deadly fire again, then dance with the girls and hoist a beer to his comrades. "When you've got it…"

Cole leaned forward, his white teeth peeking from behind his sooty face. "So come out with us tonight. You bailed the other night, and we wanna see you in action."

"I don't—"

"Unless you're afraid of some competition," another guy shouted.

"I got twenty on Kimball," Cole said.

"I wouldn't take that bet," Josh advised the others. "Especially since it would be so easy for him to hook up with an old flame."

Steve cocked his head. Who did he know—

"Laine Sheehan is in town."

His heart stuttered. He and Laine had dated the summer after her college graduation. He, Josh and Tommy had been roommates, living in Fairfax, working for the forestry service as smoke jumpers. Cocky and wild, they'd cut a now-notorious path through the parties and clubs of Redding and one night had run into Laine and some other women from Fairfax.

The shy, reserved blonde had stopped Steve dead in his tracks.

Though Josh and Tommy had never really understood his single-minded interest in Laine, Steve had soaked up her gentleness, her golden-brown eyes, her complete adoration of him. At the end of the summer he'd asked her to move in with him, but she couldn't deal with his dangerous job, and she'd gone back home to Texas.

At the time, he'd been resentful of her asking him to choose her or his job, but seven years later he supposed he understood her hesitation to get more involved with him. Especially in light of Tommy's death.

He'd never completely gotten over her.

"How do you know she's here?" he asked Josh, feeling the gazes of the other men on him.

"Saw her the other night at Suds."

Steve raised his eyebrows. "What was Laine doing at Suds?"

"Drinkin'."

"Drink—" The truck jerked to a halt before Steve could finish. Since they had to consult with forestry service officials about the fire's progress and get their schedule for the following day, he didn't have a chance to question Josh further until dinner.

As he dug into baked chicken, macaroni and cheese and green beans, he was grateful for the delicious food. The churches in Fairfax had banded together to feed the dozens of teams fighting the fires, and they'd pulled out all the stops. He didn't even want to think about any of those people losing their homes and businesses.

"So why was Laine Sheehan drinking at Suds?" he asked Josh quietly as they sat next to each other in the bustling food tent located in the base camp's center.

He shrugged. "I didn't ask, and she didn't say."

"Some help you are."

"I don't know why you're still getting worked up about that woman. You're complete opposites."

"Thank you, Dr. Phil."

"And, sorry to be critical here, but she's not up to your usual physical standards."

"Just because she doesn't have a double-D chest—"

"Though, come to think of it, she looked pretty good the other night."

Steve put down his fork. "She did? How good?"

"I don't know, man. Just good." He pushed his plate aside. "And if you're so interested, I heard she's staying out at her aunt's and covering the fire for some big-time magazine."

"Laine is covering the fire?"

"That's what I heard."

"This fire. Our fire."

"*Yes.*"

"She dumped me because she thought my job was too dangerous—"

"And don't forget she wasn't wild about your popularity with women."

"She never said that. I just got that feeling."

"I told you at the time that I agreed with you. I still do. Women can get real possessive."

"And men don't?" Steve waved away the comment before Josh, who had gotten into countless fights over some guy looking at his date, could respond. "We basically broke up over my job, and now she's covering the fire."

"Kinda weird the way life turns out, huh?"

"Does she realize she'll have to get reasonably close to the fire to take pictures of it?"

"I assume so. Laine was a quiet one, but no one could call her that naive." Josh paused. "I guess this means you're going out with us tonight."

For a minute, Steve wondered if seeing Laine

again was a good idea. He'd already spent a lot of time the last few days reflecting on the past. The path he'd taken. His regrets and mistakes.

His life had been one long adventure. As the youngest of four and the son of a firefighter tragically killed when Steve was only nine, he'd been indulged and encouraged to pursue the never-ending energy and curiosity that filled him. High school and a year at a university in Europe. Firefighter and paramedic training. Working in the Atlanta Fire Department. Then smoke jumper training and tackling one of the most challenging—and dangerous—aspects of firefighting.

Then one spring he and another firefighter had been trapped for several hours along a ridge during a wildfire. The experience spooked Steve. He'd never found the same level of commitment to smoke jumping or forest fires since. So, he'd gone back to his home in north Georgia. Though part of him felt as if he was running from fears and insecurities he didn't want to face, and that he was betraying the memory of his heroic father, he'd been happy.

He'd discovered he didn't need constant life-and-death struggles to fulfill himself. He could be satisfied keeping the women of Baxter occupied and playing cards in the firehouse in between saving cats from trees.

When adventure had tapped him on the shoulder a few days ago, offering another taste of exhilaration, he'd accepted reluctantly. He was only here to honor Tommy's memory. To offer himself to Josh and the rest of the team one last time.

Maybe Laine could remind him why he belonged with these guys. "Oh, yeah, I'm coming."

LAINE SQUINTED. Most of the bar was a vague blur.

Maybe she shouldn't have ordered a cosmopolitan then downed half the contents in one swallow. Gulping was the only way she could get the thing down. Though her sister and friends had claimed the drink as their own—as a joke, since being cosmopolitan in tiny Kendall, Texas, was something of a challenge—she'd never gotten used to the taste.

She was going to need a designated driver at this rate. And still nothing would change the humiliating call she'd gotten that afternoon from her editor.

Mac, in his charming, sweet way, had torn into her pictures. Though at least by sending the digital images, she'd assumed that he couldn't literally tear them.

"Do I need to send one of the boys out there to show you what pictures of a fire look like?" he'd asked.

She'd sent him pictures of evacuation preparations, people living in the shelters and firefighters getting into their gear. Though planning to develop a well-rounded piece—complete with uplifting shots as well as action ones—she was still working her way up to the actual fire.

"You don't need to send the boys," she'd said, not at all surprised by Mac's impatience. "I'm going up in a helicopter tomorrow."

Which was why she was drinking tonight.

Her assurances had warded off Mac's threat of replacement and kept her paycheck coming—for the moment anyway.

She sipped her cosmo, winced, then promptly advised her scaredy-cat conscience that she wasn't some insecure little girl who had nightmares about her boyfriend's horrifying death. She'd conquered her fear of heights years ago. Her hands had barely shaken as she'd watched a truckload of tired-looking smoke jumpers climb out of a chopper yesterday.

Unfortunately, her plan to take care of Aunt Jen wasn't going much better than her job. She'd tried to convince her aunt that her home was about to be consumed by fire. And wouldn't it be a good idea to be prepared for that event?

Nope. Not according to Aunt Jen. And her prayer group was working overtime just to be sure.

"Can I buy you a drink, honey?"

Scowling, she glanced up at a smiling, dark-haired man. "No, thanks."

Men were the last complication she needed. Thankfully, she hadn't seen Steve or anyone on his team yesterday, as they were deep in the forest, digging fire lines. She'd met Chief Jeff Arnold, finding him professional, experienced and cooperative.

And much more interesting than the guy who was now sitting next to her, despite her refusal of his drink offer.

"I'm Mark," he said.

Laine pushed to her feet. "I'm going."

"Don't go. Have a drink with me." Mark pointed at her half-full martini glass. "Cosmo?"

"Yes, but—"

As Mark raised his hand to catch the bartender's attention, she noticed something jaw-dropping. "You're wearing a wedding ring."

Mark shrugged. "I'm just looking for someone to talk to."

No wonder she spent her days working and her nights and weekends balancing the books at Temptation. Alone. "Are you really?"

"My wife understands."

"I'll bet."

"What can I get you?" the bartender asked.

"Nothing," Laine said before Mark could respond. Shaking her head, she waved. "Bye, Mark."

As Mark the Cheating Scumbag got up from his stool and strolled away, Laine glanced around Suds. With its ancient-looking tables, scuffed floor, ever-flowing tap and simple bar food, it reminded her of Temptation.

It was still hard to believe she was too far away to rush back to Kendall and see what problems had popped up at the bar.

She did, however, have to worry what bills might need paying. And she couldn't push aside the compulsion to call her sister and remind her to call the auction house about selling the furniture.

She'd left a clearly outlined plan of action taped to the bar before she'd left on Thursday, and she'd bet her best zoom lens that Cat hadn't so much as glanced at it.

Digging her cell phone from her purse, she called the bar. Though it was nearly nine on a Sunday night, she knew her sister wouldn't be home with a cup of tea and a book.

"Cat?" she yelled into the phone over the blaring music.

"Lainey?"

Laine ground her teeth. "Have you called the auction house yet? We need to get some cash for the furniture to pay off the liquor supplier."

"Hi, sister dear, how are you?" Cat answered back in a sarcastic tone. "How was your day? I'm sure it's *so* difficult dealing with everything *all on your own* since I left you there without a thought at all for *anybody but myself.*"

Laine eyed the bar in front of her and tried to resist the urge to pound her head against it. They'd had this argument already. Her income was all they had at the end of the month. She had to make sure the money kept coming in. "Please don't start, Cat," she said calmly. "You'll be fine. Just follow my list."

"What list?"

"The one I taped to the bar that explained step by step what you needed to do this week."

"Oh, I wondered what that was. Some guy spilled whiskey all over it Friday night. I threw it away."

Laine rubbed her temples. Why had she called? Why did she continue to submit herself to the torture of communicating with her sister? "I'll e-mail you another copy. And call the auction house first thing tomorrow."

"I'm busy."

"Please, Cat. We have to get moving on these things."

"Yeah, sure *we* do."

Was that a catch in her sister's voice? Okay, maybe she was irresponsible and forgetful, but she was family. Her baby sister. This closing was hard on her. Maybe—

"Look, Laine, I've got to go," she said and disconnected.

Their once-boisterous Irish father was no doubt rolling over in his grave at the tension between his two girls. Laine had always taken care of her sister, tried to get her to do the right thing, the responsible thing. But Cat never saw things the same way and inevitably dug in her heels whenever Laine tried to convince her otherwise.

Feeling both relief at having done her duty and overwhelming guilt at abandoning Cat to tasks she would never manage on her own, she closed her cell phone, then dropped it back in her purse.

She would just have to straighten it all out when she got back.

Rolling her shoulders, she thought about her shooting plan for the next day. Some aerials of the damage, some—

Without fanfare or a drumroll, Steve Kimball walked into the bar, his buddy Josh Burke flanking him.

Steve looked every bit as good as he had that summer. Wavy black hair, broad shoulders, confident, seductive smile. Caught up in her stunned, drooling stare, she even thought—from fifteen feet away—she could see the mischievous glint in his bright blue eyes.

Her body loosened. Sparked. Stood at attention.

Though confused at being awakened so suddenly, she was pretty sure her libido saluted.

What had she done? Why had she thought she

could be within twenty miles of this man and not want him again?

Like the chicken she was trying to prove she wasn't, she hid behind a menu. She wasn't ready to face him.

By now she supposed he knew she was in town, since she'd spotted Josh the first night she'd arrived, when she'd met her friend Denise for drinks.

As she peeked past the menu, she saw him looking around the bar, as if searching for someone. Her? Not likely. He'd been angry and resentful when she'd asked him to choose between her and his job. In retrospect, she could hardly blame him.

An adventurer like him wouldn't have stayed satisfied with her for long. Not when he had his pick of any woman he wanted. And she couldn't imagine spending her life watching him jump out of airplanes, wondering when the day would come that he never made it home.

Deep down she'd known they'd never last. Asking him to choose, when she already knew the answer, was an easy way to bring everything to a neat end.

He and Josh obviously spotted their buddies in a back booth, already crowded with giggling women. She recalled many times when Steve, Josh and Tommy were surrounded by women. Josh, with his shaggy, curly dark hair and direct stare. Tommy with his clean-cut, blond California good looks. And Steve, rounding out the gorgeous and charming threesome.

She could hardly blame the women for their good taste. Still, Laine had been embarrassingly insecure and jealous.

In the years since, she'd grown up a lot, found some confidence and backbone. She wasn't emotionally invested in Steve anymore. He and his dangerous job simply reminded her of an uncertain time in her life, and of her insecurity about his feelings for her. And while he might still affect her body, his job didn't matter, except in relation to her photo assignment. She wasn't falling for him again.

Especially since he wasn't likely to give her a second glance.

Save Aunt Jen from a wildfire and her pride. Wow her editor with action, nongirlie photos. Resist Steve Kimball.

A workable plan. A reasonable plan.

Right?

2

SETTLED INTO A BOOTH and surrounded by Josh and Cole and the lovely ladies they'd invited, Steve glanced around the bar. He saw several colleagues, a few people he vaguely recalled from either his residency seven years ago or the recent work on the fires, plus a stranger or two.

Certainly no Laine Sheehan.

He wished he wasn't so disappointed. They hadn't parted on the best of terms. It's not as though she'd be holding up a welcome banner.

"So, did you put out the fire yet?" a buxom brunette sitting between Josh and Cole asked.

"No, silly," her equally buxom blond companion said with a nudge. "Don't you ever watch the news?"

"Not if I can help it…"

Steve let their voices fade into the background. Though he hesitated to admit it to himself, and certainly wouldn't tell his friends, he was bored.

And he couldn't explain why. Back home in Georgia he liked nothing better than to hang out with his buddies from the firehouse. If a woman or two wandered across his path, all the better.

Why was he restless? Why could he only manage a smile at Cole's raunchy joke?

Simple. He couldn't get Laine out of his mind.

"You all right?" Cole asked.

"Fine." He sipped his beer. "It's just been a helluva few days."

"Tell me about it. This is a wild one."

"You ever feel like you're just barely hangin' on?"

"All the time." Cole reached for a handful of beer nuts. "It's good to have you back, though. Tommy would have loved it."

"Yeah. It's not the same without him." And Steve wondered if the knot in his stomach would ever loosen. "You think we can beat this thing?"

"Hell yeah. And it'll sure be fun trying."

Steve forced himself to smile, knowing the facade of enthusiasm he had to keep up. "Sure will."

Josh pushed the pitcher of beer their way. "Thank God the workday's done."

Cole refilled their mugs. "And the night's young."

Steve clanged his mug against the others', caught the gaze of the brunette who didn't watch the news, then looked away. Hanging with his old buddies again helped him accept Tommy's death, and even made him recall his exhilarating days as a smoke jumper without panicking. But part of him also realized he'd moved on. Running, but still on to something new.

As he sipped his beer, he caught a glimpse of a blonde at the far end of the bar, a black camera bag resting by her feet. "Laine?" he said aloud, though nobody likely heard him over the toasts.

He rose. "I'll be back," he said absently to Cole, leaving his beer on the table and keeping his gaze locked on the familiar woman across the room.

She looked nearly the same. Lovely. Delicate, but strong. Wearing jeans, a crewneck white shirt and navy blazer, she didn't seem ordinary in the ordinary clothes. Instead of the ponytail he remembered, her hair fell to her shoulders and curved softly around her face. Her lips, which he always remembered her biting, were full and glossy pink.

He stopped next to her and felt a familiar desire slide into his stomach. "Hi, Laine."

"Hi, Steve," she said, her brown-eyed gaze meeting his dead on.

This close, something about her, the look in her eyes, or the strength of her posture, made her seem bolder, more confident. Though he'd been crazy about shy and sweet Laine, he found himself drawn to the change.

Oh, yeah, rekindling the heat between him and Laine could be just the thing to jolt him out of his depression and distract him from the duty he dreaded.

He loomed over her and liked the way her eyes widened at his proximity. "Can an old friend buy you a drink?"

"Sure." Cool as a cucumber, she shrugged. "If you can fit me into your fan club. Maybe you should give everybody membership numbers. You know, to keep things fair."

The old tension returned as though seven minutes had passed rather than seven years. He couldn't help it if people felt comfortable approaching him. He was a firefighter and well known in Fairfax. His height communicated confidence. Hell, people *liked* him. Was that a crime?

"I don't have a fan club," he said.

She winked. "Right."

He realized she was teasing. Of course she wouldn't still be carrying around seven-year-old jealousy. "Hey, we've been in the woods for two days."

"So I hear." She patted the empty stool next to her, her smile dispelling the gloom that had settled over him that afternoon. "Have a seat."

Steve swallowed. *Why does she make me so weak?*

He stepped toward her, stopping just short of his chest brushing her back as he settled onto the stool. A spicy, fruity scent washed over him, and his body hardened.

"You look really beautiful." In fact, he had to curl his hands into fists to keep from stroking her shoulder.

"Thanks." She grinned. "So do you."

Ridiculously, he felt his face heat. "Thanks. Josh told me you're covering the fire for some major magazine."

"Yeah. I signed on with *Century.*"

He whistled. "I'm honored to think I was part of the test photos."

"I do still have one of you in my portfolio."

"No kidding?"

"Yeah. One of you, Josh and Tommy stumbling out of a plane after you'd just come off a two-day wildfire on the California–Oregon border."

His heart lurched.

"I heard about Tommy," she said quietly. "I'm so sorry. What happened?"

Oddly enough, despite her aversion to his job, it felt right sharing his pain with her. "The fire. A sudden wind."

She closed her eyes briefly. When she opened them again, tears clung to her lashes. Her compassion reminded him why he'd fallen so hard. "Are you okay?"

He didn't want to face his grief for Tommy now. He'd been wallowing in it for a week. He slid his hand around her waist. "I'm better now."

She leaned back and gave him a wry look. "And still smooth as ever."

Smiling, he gripped her side. "Why am I thinking that's not a compliment?"

"But it is. And especially convenient for the available ladies of Fairfax."

"And do you include yourself in that group?"

"Definitely not."

Damn. "You're married?"

"No. Just not available."

"To me?"

"To anybody." She polished off the pink contents of her martini glass. "Another cosmo, please," she said to the smiling young bartender who appeared before her.

Steve ordered a beer. "Since when do you drink cosmos?"

"I have for years."

Something was definitely up with a cosmo-drinking, sassy-mouthed, unavailable Laine. *It's been seven years, man. People change. Look at you.*

He was challenged by her lack of interest in him. Because he was still interested in her? Or because she'd once been so dedicated to him?

Either way, it was probably a good idea to back off. At least for the moment. "How's Aunt Jen?"

"Stubborn as ever. She doesn't want to leave her house."

"She may not have to."

"Chief Arnold seemed to think differently when I was at base camp yesterday. You really believe she won't need to leave?"

"We're supposed to be thinking positively on the front line, but no. Evacuations will happen." He accepted his beer from the bartender; Laine did the same with her cosmo. "If we don't get some rain soon, the town is right in the fire's path."

She held up her glass. "Then a toast to rain. To Tommy." Pausing, she met his gaze. "And to the rest of you staying safe."

He tapped his mug against her glass. "To Tommy." He wasn't toasting himself. The reluctance he felt at every jump, every trip into the ravaged forest, made a mockery of the other teams' bravery.

She sipped her drink, then puckered her lips and set the glass aside.

"Too strong?"

"No, it's…fine. So, how've you been?"

He drank his beer, figuring at least they'd agree on the changes he'd made in his life. "I gave up smoke jumping and moved back home to Georgia a few years ago."

Laine nearly fell off her stool. "You—*What?*"

"I went home, joined a regular firehouse, started saving cats from trees. I even bought a house."

She couldn't grasp it. "What about parachuting from planes into fire-choked forests? What about rappelling from helicopters? What about Italy and Greece? You had hiking, biking, scuba diving and who knows what else planned."

"The farthest I've been from home in the last four years is Atlanta."

Bad boy Steve had reformed? Settled down? Good grief.

"Did you get married?" she asked, still stunned enough to wonder what else she'd missed.

"No."

"Have any kids?"

Leaning toward her, he grinned. "No. Are you volunteering?"

That brought back painful memories. When she'd been young and wide-eyed. When she'd thought she and Steve would get married someday, have a family together. Instead, he'd asked her to move in and made it clear he planned to be a smoke jumper until he was old and gray.

Going back there wouldn't help, and she really didn't want to go several rounds with him over the past. "But you *are* here working on the fires."

"My old team called me when Tommy died. They asked me to fill in."

He'd probably left home with skid marks. *Settled down? No way.* "And it's great to be back."

He drank his beer. "Oh, yeah."

See, nothing had changed, her heart reminded her.

And even though her libido protested, she told herself that was a *good* thing. She didn't want to want Steve. She had a job to do. A paycheck to maintain. An aunt to battle.

Still, she couldn't deny how good it felt to sit next to him again. His wild, mischievous smile and confidence had thrown her for a loop from the beginning, but she'd soon learned there was much more beneath his beautiful face and body. He spoke three languages, had spent several years abroad, had a love of art and culture—and never passed up the opportunity to help little old ladies cross the street.

On top of her conflicting feelings, she was baffled by him flirting with her. Did he really want to pick up where they'd left off?

No way. Not a good idea. Her heart had taken too severe a beating the first time around.

"So you're just back for the fire?"

"Yeah. My life is in Georgia now."

"I thought your hometown was pretty small."

"It is."

"Not much action for an adventurous guy like yourself."

"We get our share. Had a serial arsonist running loose last fall. That was pretty exciting."

Action aplenty, even in rural Georgia. She'd been through wild, dangerous and adventurous with him before and hadn't enjoyed the results. Now she needed those qualities in him for her assignment. How ironic was that?

"How about dinner tomorrow?" he asked suddenly, leaning close to her.

"Uh...no."

"No?"

"Look, I'm sure we'll run into each other over the next few days," she said, leaning back. "And I'm sorry I kidded you with the fan-club crack earlier, but you have plenty of women lining up, so—"

"There's no line."

"Oh, they'll come. Probably the ones at that table in the back that were glaring at me a few minutes ago."

"Laine, nobody's glaring at—"

"Hi, Steve."

A curvy redhead stood next to him, her hand on her hip, her impressive chest thrown out.

Laine smirked at him before he turned to the other woman.

"Hi, Darla. Laine, do you know Darla?"

"No." Laine waved and smiled. After all, her point had been made. "Hi."

Darla smiled weakly in return, then focused on Steve. "Wasn't dinner great the other night?"

"Yeah. Thanks for going to all that trouble. The guys on the team really appreciate the effort everyone in town has made for us."

Steve's neck had turned red. He looked uncomfortable at sharing a drink with one woman while talking to another.

Darla finally drifted away, and Steve turned back to her. "Sorry about that. She and some friends made dinner for our jump team a few nights ago and—"

"Hi, Steve."

Laine bit her lip to keep from laughing.

This time the woman was a striking brunette with a sultry voice and, again, some impressive curves.

"Hi, Vivian. Do you know Laine?"

Vivian didn't bother to do more than raise her eyebrows at Laine's wave.

"We missed you Friday night," she said to Steve.

"I was exhausted."

Laine propped her chin on her fist and noticed a petite redhead waving at her from across the bar. Denise?

She had met fun, impulsive Denise the summer she'd lived in Fairfax. Her family lived next door to Aunt Jen. She and Denise had been together the night she'd met Steve in a Redding bar, had become great friends and stayed in touch ever since. Denise had come home to help her parents in case they needed to evacuate and, the night Laine arrived, caught her up on all the gossip over drinks.

She was the perfect escape from Steve.

"Excuse me," Laine said. "I see somebody I need to speak to. Why don't you two catch up."

Steve stood, and Vivian's eyes lit like sparklers. Clearly, she thought she'd scared Laine off.

As Laine's feet hit the floor, Steve wrapped his hand around her wrist. "You're coming back, right?"

Laine resisted the urge to fan herself at the intense, questioning look in his eyes. The man did know how to push her buttons. "I should go. I have to get up early…"

Steve scooped her camera bag off the floor and laid it on her empty stool. "I'll just hang on to this till you get back."

Holding her camera hostage? That was a new one. She really didn't understand his insistence, especially with the likes of Vivian about, but she did want to talk to him about some shots of him and his jump team. Which she would do—briefly—before calling it a night.

"I'll be back," she said finally.

Vivian scowled. Steve smiled.

Crossing the bar, she stopped next to Denise, who hugged her tight. "I see the subject research is going well. Nobody else I'd rather see pictures of than Steve Kimball. Any chance of catching him naked?"

"No."

Her eyes twinkled. "Please?"

Laine was having a hard time resisting the man's charm when he was clothed. No way was she picturing him naked. "Definitely not. There's nothing between us anymore."

She frowned, her dark blue eyes narrowing. "Not even a spark?"

"Mmm...well, I wouldn't say that. Did you know he'd moved?" She brought Denise up to date on Steve's switch to hometown guy, who fought fires started by arsonists, rather than jumping from planes on a daily basis.

"All that danger and excitement sounds fun to me."

"Not when you're the one left at home wondering if you'll ever see him again."

"Good point." She angled her head, her bright red curls brushing her cheek. "I hadn't heard he left Fairfax, but then I'd left for graduate school, and I didn't ask a lot of questions about him after you guys broke up." She glanced across the bar at the man in question. "He certainly hasn't lost his touch."

Laine followed her friend's stare and noted that Vivian was leaning close enough to the man to breast-feed him. A surprising pang of envy hit her.

"Vivian was always obvious," Denise said, shaking her head. "In fact, at Honors Choir tryouts—"

"Let's stay in this decade, please."

"Yeah, sure. I still don't see how you're going to follow him around taking pictures and not be tempted."

"I'll manage. Why do you think he's always surrounded?"

"He's drop-dead gorgeous, Laine. Are you sure you're feeling okay?"

"I was just hoping it was me. He's aged, after all."

"He has?"

He had. And somehow looked even better. *Men!*

"He might be worth the risk—heartbreakwise," Denise added. "I'd go for the direct approach. Invite him to your place, see where things go."

"Invite him—" She shook her head. "I don't think so. My place is Aunt Jen's."

"So go to his place."

"The only place I'm going with him is professionally related."

"Speaking of your job…how are you going to cover this fire and not actually, you know, be there?"

"Remember how I told you I'd hoped to convince my editor this was a human-interest piece?"

"Yeah."

"He's interested in humans all right. As long as a big, raging wildfire is in the background."

"Yikes."

Laine sighed. "Tell me about it." Recording action on film was great, but participating wasn't her strong point. Up until a few months ago, her biggest challenge had been figuring out the difference between a hybrid tea rose and a floribunda.

Now, no matter how terrified she was, she had to face the fire. Literally. How Steve did so on a daily basis—in the forest or in his hometown—she'd never understand. So, it was time to earn her precious paycheck, stop talking and start snapping. "I'm going to take some aerial shots in the morning."

"If you say so…"

She rolled her shoulders. "Okay. I'm going."

"Aerial shots now? It's dark."

"Not now. I've got to get my camera out of hock first."

Her stomach fluttered like crazy, no matter how many times she told herself to calm down. Thanks to Denise, images of Steve in various states of nakedness kept dancing across her mind. Memories she'd long forgotten. Or so she thought.

Distracted, she didn't notice a different woman stood by Steve until she was a few feet away. She had shoulder-length dark hair and striking turquoise eyes and a shoulder holster peaking from beneath her jacket. She looked extremely annoyed.

"Come on, lover boy," she was saying to Steve. "We were supposed to meet an hour ago, and I don't have much time."

Laine cleared her throat and crossed her arms over her chest. *These chicks are amazing.* She glanced at Steve. "*You* need a better appointment calendar."

"No, she's not— She's my sister-in-law."

Laine widened her eyes.

Rising, Steve rubbed his temples. "Cara, would you please explain what you're doing here?"

"We had a consult on the arson aspect of the wildfire," she said in a clipped, no-nonsense tone Laine admired. "I've worked on several suspiciously started forest fires over the years, and my boss, the governor of Georgia, went to school with your commanding officer, so he sent me. I talked to the guys at the site when Steve didn't show up. They said to try here." Her gaze slid over Laine, as well as the half-finished drinks on the bar. "Where you don't seem to be thinking about the fire. Sorry about that."

"No, *I'm* sorry," Steve said. "I forgot you came in yesterday. Laine, this is Cara Kimball. Cara, Laine Sheehan."

Laine shook the other woman's hand, finally realizing what her presence meant. "So, which brother did you marry?"

"Wes."

Mmm. That made sense. Though she'd only met Wes once when he'd visited Steve, she remembered him being tough and temperamental. Not a man for a meek woman. "Congratulations," she said to Cara.

"Cara is a captain in the arson division," Steve put in. "She and Wes met during a case last fall."

"So arson or careless campers with this wildfire?" Laine asked.

"Careless campers started it, but there's a possibility arsonists are egging the blaze on," Cara said.

Laine shook her head. "That doesn't exactly restore your faith in humanity."

"Hang out with me for a few days and my cases would completely destroy your faith in humanity."

Steve frowned, and Laine wondered whether he was disturbed by the content of their conversation or the chumminess between her and Cara. As Steve pulled out the stool on the other side of him, Laine waggled her finger, indicating that he should move down so she and Cara could sit next to one another.

"Join us," she said to her new friend.

Dropping onto the stool, Cara shrugged. "For a few minutes. I have to get back to work." She leaned forward and directed her attention to Steve. "And so does he."

"How could I forget?" He raised his hand to the bartender, then asked Cara what she wanted.

"Diet Coke," she said.

"One for me, too," Laine added, pushing her martini glass aside.

"Ben got married recently, too," Cara said.

"Really?" Ever since the death of Steve's father, Ben had been the leader of the Kimball clan. Laine had never met him, but she'd gotten the impression that Ben was both reserved and revered. A longtime role model for Steve.

"Steve's the last bachelor in the family," Cara said, cutting her gaze toward her brother-in-law. "And likely to stay that way."

"Certainly not from a lack of available candidates."

"None of them seem to hold his interest for more than a couple of months, though."

Laine nodded. "Been there."

"No kidding? You and Steve?"

"Yep. About seven years ago. For a couple of months during the summer."

Cara shook her head. "The story of his life."

"I'm right here, you know," Steve said, sounding annoyed.

Without looking at him, Laine patted his hand. "And we're glad to have you."

"Why do you think he never hangs around very long?" she asked Cara.

"You know men. They can never turn down a buffet." She glanced at Steve. "Not that it's any of my business."

"Oh, right. Not mine either." She slid off her stool and scooped her camera bag off the floor. Though she'd gotten caught up in her rapport with Cara, she didn't have any interest in or right to Steve's personal life. "I'd like to take some pictures of you both in action this week, if you don't mind."

"Laine is a photographer for *Century* magazine," Steve said to Cara as he rose.

"I'd rather not have most of what I'm doing recorded," Cara said, scowling. "Except by me. Sorry."

Laine liked the idea of a female arson investigator in the middle of the disaster. And she thought Cara's intense personality would come across dramatically in the pictures. "I'll let you see any photos I'm considering for publication. You'll have the opportunity to sign—or not sign—a release."

"I'll consider it," Cara said.

"Great." She looked up at Steve, ignoring the warmth flooding her body. "I'd like to shoot you and Josh and the others, too. When's your next day on-site?"

"The day after tomorrow—Tuesday."

Laine shook Steve's hand. "I'll see you then, I guess."

3

STEVE RESISTED THE URGE to pound his head against the bar. Handshakes? *I'll see you then, I guess?*

Could he be losing his touch?

As Laine strode away, Steve held up his finger and said to Cara, "I'll be right back."

He caught up with Laine just outside the bar. Had he said something to himself about *liking* the challenge she presented? He must have gone temporarily insane.

Yes, he had. Insane with need for Laine.

The memory of her. The reality of her. The reminder of the man he'd once been. Strong. Brave. Fearless.

"How about dinner tomorrow?" he asked again when she looked up at him as if wondering why he was following her down the sidewalk.

"No."

"I'm not a smoke jumper anymore."

"Really?" She stopped and crossed her arms over her chest. "And how did you get to the site of that ridge fire two days ago? Stroll leisurely into the forest with Bambi and the rest of the gentle woodland creatures?"

She had a point there. "Okay, so I'm *temporarily* a smoke jumper. But only until this fire is out."

"Then you go back to Georgia, and I go back to Texas."

He slid his thumb along her jawline. "But while we're here…"

"I'll be working. You'll be working."

"Not all the time."

She stepped back, away from his touch. A light of determination appeared in her eyes that he'd never seen before—at least not until the day she'd dumped him. "I'm not doing this again, Steve. Smoke jumper or not, nothing has changed."

"We were great together before. What's wrong with trying to find that again?"

"You asked me to move in with you while you were in the hospital recovering from smoke inhalation."

When he'd been selfish and caught up in the adventure of his job, she'd been there, staring at him with her big brown eyes, offering her quiet devotion. Now, when he realized that he'd lost—her gentleness, her ability to be quiet and still, and not always running from one adventure to another, she wanted nothing to do with him. "Not exactly my best timing."

"You've got my agreement there. I also recall a fire down South. You were supposed to meet me for dinner and showed up three hours late. And for two of those hours, I couldn't find anyone who could tell me whether you were dead or alive."

Steve winced. "I know. Josh—"

"Dragged you off to a celebratory drink at a local bar. I remember."

He dragged his hand through his hair. "This isn't going at all like I planned."

"I imagine not. But you're still a firefighter, and I've learned from my mistakes."

Was that what their relationship had been? A mistake? Is that how she remembered him?

The idea rankled his pride, and landed a powerful blow on the wonderful past with her that he cherished. And while he couldn't deny that he didn't want to go back to smoke jumping, and this trip to California brought up bad memories of wildfires, he'd kicked down many doors of burning houses and buildings in his life. He couldn't see that ever changing.

"You have a line of women who want you," she continued. "You don't want me."

"I do."

"Maybe you just want the memory of me. I'm not the same quiet girl I was seven years ago."

He clenched his fists by his sides. "No, that's not it. We're not just a memory."

Or a mistake.

He tugged her hand, pulling her down the sidewalk and around the corner of the building. Wide-eyed, she stared at him as if she understood something inside him had just shifted. When he moved closer to her, she backed up. "And knowing all that, you still want me," he said.

She laid her hands against his chest. "Maybe we still have some physical chemistry, but—"

He pressed his hips against hers, trapping her against the brick building. "You're really beautiful. Have I told you that?"

"Earlier, I seem to recall—"

He kissed her jaw, just below her ear, where—at least in the past—he'd made her shiver and moan. "I think we should pick up where we left off…"

She sighed, leaning her head to the side, giving him better access.

He'd forgotten how silky and delicious her skin was. As he cupped the back of her head, he closed his eyes, inhaling the fruity scent clinging to her that was somehow sweet and exotic.

Suddenly, she pushed him back. "Where we left off, huh? We left off at a big fight, where you told me you had adventures and challenges to tackle and had no plans to give up your certain-death job."

"I've changed my mind about that, you know." He pulled her into his arms, nuzzling her neck.

"It doesn't look that way to me."

He dragged his lips across her cheek. "Give me a chance to show you."

"I shouldn't."

"But you will." Sensing her will weakening, he captured her mouth with his own, sighing into the warmth and curves of her body. He slid his tongue past her lips, hungering for more of her, desperate for her response.

And, not sure how telling that revelation was, he angled his head, seeking to draw more from her, to absorb her need with his own.

Heat from her body infused his. Desire crashed over him as if it had only been lying dormant over the years, just waiting to pounce and grab him by the throat.

With just the edge of the floodlights illuminating them, Laine's body was part flesh, part shadow. Crushed against his chest, her nipples hardened, and he envisioned her lying back, her arms outstretched, him on top of her, yanking her clothes from her body.

She tasted familiar, but seemed different. She met his hunger with confidence, not shying away an inch from his intense desire. He took his time relearning her lips, the best angle for their heads, the curve at the small of her back, the swell of her backside.

A piercing whistle broke through the quiet of the night.

Then he heard Cara's voice. "I've cooled my heels long enough, Steve. Get your ass back in here."

Laine froze. "What have I—" Smoothing her hair back into place and clutching her camera bag to her side, she ducked beneath his arm. "I have to go."

Steve's chest was still heaving, his body still throbbing.

It's the pursuit. It has to be the pursuit.

Laine was the only woman within three blocks who hadn't come on to him. That's the only reason he wanted her so much. Pretty stupid. And childish.

He had work to do here. He needed to put all his effort and concentration in jumping out of planes, rappelling from helicopters and plunging headlong into flames and smoke every day. He didn't have time to be distracted by women, especially Laine.

But he still wanted her so much. The sense that he'd screwed up big by letting her go seven years ago washed over him, stronger than ever.

Her face flushed, and waggling her fingers, she scooted back. "See you around, Steve."

"Count on it," he muttered as he watched her walk away.

HER STOMACH IN KNOTS, Laine climbed into the helicopter's passenger seat.

Remember, this is your job…

With his aviator sunglasses in place, the pilot gave her a reassuring smile. She hoped she didn't throw up on his shoes.

A forestry official gave her a headset and strapped her in, then he closed the door. Laine shut her eyes as the helicopter began to lift from the ground.

Are you crazy? You're a photographer, not Lara Croft.

She'd reluctantly been up in helicopters before, photographing the grounds at the Biltmore Estate and the progress of the Rose Bowl Parade. Once she got over the initial takeoff, she'd always been able to manage her fear if she focused on the view through her lens.

She liked the solitude and silence of photography. She liked the ability to change what she saw and how she saw it. She liked capturing moments in time, reflecting on them hours, days and years later.

She gripped the sides of her seat to steady her rolling stomach as the chopper banked.

"I have a one-hundred-percent success rate," said a disembodied voice through her headset.

She glanced over at the pilot and gave him a weak thumbs-up. She tried not to focus on the height, the noise of the whirring blades, the fact that she was thousands of feet in the air and supported by a bit of glass and metal and a five-point safety harness.

And after taking a deep breath, she managed to look out the windshield.

They were high over the forest and mountains now, turning trees into twigs and cars into model toys.

The scorched blackness of much of the area made her throat tighten. From the research she'd done on wildfires, she knew smaller ones that didn't threaten civilization were allowed a controlled burn. This cleansing of the land was actually good for the environment and encouraged new growth.

But destruction of this magnitude was disastrous. The fire was now ripping through a stretch of land where a developer had built a collection of cabins he rented out to companies for management retreats. Small, "hot spot" fires sparked by the larger blaze were popping up all over the area. Wildlife homes were reduced to ashes. A small park and series of hiking trails that were owned and managed by the forestry service had been destroyed.

And Fairfax was next on the list.

Spurred by that threat, she pulled out her digital camera, with its high-powered zoom lens, to record the scene. As the pilot swung as low as was safe over the blaze, she realized the fire was beautiful, in its way. The colors, the power and the heat were mesmerizing, as well as deadly.

The pilot set them down once near a small hot spot, where Laine was able to get out and take some close-ups of the crew.

She forgot about her own fears as she watched

them dig trenches and clear trees and brush to rob the fire of fuel, then aid that effort with extinguishing chemicals. They sweated and strained. Through her fireproof jumpsuit and without the heavy supply pack most of the crew carried, Laine could hardly stay coherent in the heat. Still, she had to stifle the urge to grab a shovel and help.

They were an amazing breed, these men and women who challenged a force of nature that only God himself could really battle and win. It was an alliance Steve was an integral part of, and one she didn't think she'd ever fully understand.

On the flight back to base camp, as she made observational notes and got estimates of damaged acres from the pilot, she saw another helicopter flying in the distance, directly into the billowing smoke.

"Smoke jumpers," the pilot said, pointing at the chopper.

She swallowed. "They're not parachuting?"

"As of this morning they were able to land the helicopter in the forest like we did. They're working with the hotshot crews on the ground and actually jumping only on a limited basis, to put out stray fires in more rugged areas."

She turned her head. She remembered that change in strategy from other fires Steve had fought. Somehow it didn't ease her mind.

Despite her efforts all morning to avoid thinking about Steve, a vision of him popped into her head anyway.

She shivered with remembrance at his kiss. All that fire and need and muscle. The man heated her blood and sent her body into a raging hunger that hadn't dampened one bit in the years they'd been apart.

She'd run smack into a dangerous bad boy. Again. The kind she was supposed to run from. The kind that wasn't good for her heart. Or peace of mind.

Bad boys all led to heartbreak. Her sister always forgot the last one that had made her cry and went back to them, but Laine wasn't going down that road again.

On the ground, she thanked the pilot, resisted the urge to kiss the dirt beneath her feet and strode into the common-area tent where meals were served.

And ran into the one person she'd hoped to avoid.

She whirled, tossing coffee in an arc as he walked up behind her. "Steve."

He stood close to her, his arms crossed over his broad chest. "How was the flight?"

Her knees were going weak. "Fine. Just fine."

"I thought you were scared of heights."

"Uh, not anymore."

He nodded at her camera bag. "This seems a long way from deer and squirrels."

She recalled him finding her study of wildlife boring. In fact, the one time she'd brought him out with her, he'd thought the woods were a much better place for seduction than photography. "I guess so. And everything's digital now. I could instantly bore you with my slide shows."

"Your slide shows didn't bore me."

"Yes, they did."

He glanced at the ground, then back at her. "I'm sorry. I didn't mean to hurt your feelings." He grinned, stepping closer, so that their bodies were just an inch from touching. "Maybe it was just the subject matter. Now, if those pictures had been self-portraits...you would have had my full attention."

How did he always manage to do that? Turn the conversation to a subject that threw her off and made her forget why she'd been annoyed with him? "My pilot said you guys weren't jumping as much."

"Yeah. We're usually able to land the chopper or rappel down."

"Rappel—" She stopped, closing her eyes briefly as a vision of that scooted across her mind. "How...efficient." His personal safety was none of her business anymore, she reminded herself. "So why are you here?"

"Because I heard you were here."

The deep timbre of his voice sent desire skating down her spine. She fought against the feeling. He couldn't do this to her again. Make her feel as if all his considerable energy and concentration were focused exclusively on her.

She smiled, hoping she made it convincingly forced. "How sweet."

"I wanted to see you."

"Why?"

"Not much to do between jumps."

"Not much to—" She stopped, considering. "You're messing with me now."

"That's what *you* think *I* think."

She really didn't like how he'd turned that around on her. "Maybe."

As his gaze locked with hers, he took her empty foam cup. "That's not what I'm thinking."

Oh, hell, those eyes are too beautiful. Was she crazy? Could she really resist him indefinitely?

He turned and refilled her cup, added powdered creamer and artificial sweetener, just the way she liked it.

She took the coffee and sipped. Despite occasionally getting waylaid by Josh and his other buddies, he'd always been considerate and thoughtful. On top of his physical effect on her, wasn't *that* just the last thing she needed to be reminded of?

And she still couldn't resist probing his thoughts. "So, what are *you* thinking?"

"When I want to share, I'll let you know."

"Are you trying to piss me off?"

"Kissing you sure didn't help things. I thought I'd try a new strategy."

She didn't want him using *any* strategy on her. But admitting that seemed like a mistake.

He filled his own cup, which he drank black. Why in the world they were drinking coffee when it was so hot and dry she had no idea, but at least the caffeine gave her sleep-deprived body a boost. She hadn't slept well since realizing Temptation would really close and the financial strain she and her sister would soon be under. The dread of her flight today and seeing Steve again hadn't exactly helped.

"The fire doesn't look anywhere near contained," she said to direct the conversation to something professional.

"It isn't," Steve said. "We're going to start evacuating tomorrow."

"Where?"

"Some outlying properties. One neighborhood. Your aunt is safe—for now." He looked off into the distance. "Nothing we do makes any difference. The wind keeps shifting, the fire spreads to new areas. And the ground was dry as dust before all this started."

"We need rain."

"Laine?"

Laine glanced over at the approaching man, dressed in green army fatigue pants and a T-shirt, his dark brown hair sprinkled with silver. He looked tired and frustrated but gave them a warm smile.

"Chief," Steve said, nodding with respect.

Laine extended her hand. "Hi, Jeff."

"How did the shoot go this morning?"

"Good. I really appreciate you accommodating me."

"Just make sure I get copies."

Laine patted her camera bag. "I got some great aerial shots today I think you'll like." She turned her attention to Steve. "Jeff asked me to share my pictures with him for research and training."

"Good idea, sir," Steve said.

"Except for the infrared photos, I never think much about documenting. I usually leave that to the newspaper people. But them I don't trust. Laine I do."

Steve's gaze slid to hers. "She's definitely trustworthy."

How did he make that simple, professional statement sound erotic? Oh, she was *way* out of her league.

"You guys ought to come to the seminar tonight at the Fairfax Town Hall."

"Seminar?" Laine asked absently, still staring at Steve.

"Disaster preparedness. We'll have experts address the issue of saving critical documents—medical records, birth certificates, passports, insurance papers. Plus, people from law enforcement, the fire department, forestry service and hospitals. I'm sure Steve told you about the evacuations. We need to prepare the town."

Laine reminded herself that she was here to work, not drool over Steve. From the scene the chief described, she'd already set up imaginary shots in her mind. "I'd love to come," she said to Jeff. "What time?"

"Seven." He turned as someone called his name. "Thanks, Laine. I'll see you tonight." He jogged off toward a group of green–clad forestry officials who'd gathered at the edge of the tent.

"Jeff, huh?"

Laine glanced back toward Steve, noticing a bead of sweat roll down his bicep. She resisted the urge to fan herself. When did it get so stinkin' hot?

"I never even knew the chief's first name until now," he continued.

Jealous? But she immediately wiped that thought away. She couldn't imagine Steve being insecure about anything. "I should go," she said as she backed up. "I promised to bring Aunt Jen lunch."

"I haven't eaten lunch, either. How about if I join you?"

"You're inviting yourself to lunch?"

"Yes." He smiled. "Besides, I haven't even seen Aunt Jen."

"So?"

"She always liked me."

AUNT JEN, WHO HAD a different version of small-town hospitality than just about everyone else Laine knew, looked Steve up and down. "Who's this?"

Laine glanced at Steve, who shifted the lunch bags. His confident smile wavered a bit. "Steve Kimball," she explained to her aunt. "We dated that summer I lived with you while you recovered from knee surgery, remember?"

Aunt Jen narrowed her brown eyes and planted her hands on her trim hips. Her silver hair, which she always wore in a tight bun, added to the severity of her stance. "Is he the one who climbed up the trellis and squashed my roses?"

Laine choked as she held back a start of surprise. "How do you know—"

"Hmmph. I'm half-blind, girl, but I'm not deaf." She turned and headed down the hall toward the kitchen.

"'*She always liked me*,'" Laine repeated softly to Steve. "Uh-huh."

"Maybe I should offer to replace her rosebush."

Laine shook her head. "She'll just think you're sucking up."

"I am."

"Keep thinking positive. Maybe she'll join your fan club."

"I don't have a fan—"

"What's this?" Laine asked as she ground to a halt just inside the kitchen.

Aunt Jen grabbed a large bag from the pile just inside the back door and started dragging it across the floor. "What's it look like?"

"Sandbags," Laine said, frowning.

Steve laid the lunch on the table, then crossed to Jen. "Sit down," he said, drawing her away from the heavy bag. "I'll do this."

Considerate, thoughtful, even heroic. How am I supposed to fight this?

Laine shook aside her distracting thoughts and glared at her aunt, who promptly ignored her and began poking in the lunch bags. "Why are you lining the room with sandbags?"

Aunt Jen drew out a cheeseburger wrapped in paper. "Ooh, Louie's. My favorite." She peered back in the bag. "Where's the fries?"

"No fries. You're supposed to be watching your fat and cholesterol." She'd hesitated about the burgers, too, but compromised with herself by thinking about the grilled chicken and steamed vegetables she planned to make for dinner.

Aunt Jen sniffed in derision. "Doctors. Spoilsports is more like it. I don't wanna live a long life if I gotta spend it eatin' lettuce and carrots every day."

Laine ignored her aunt's bad attitude and focused on the sandbags, which Steve was dutifully lining around the room. "Would you stop?" she snapped at him. Sighing, she leaned on the table. "The bags, Aunt Jen? What are you doing with them?"

She rolled her eyes. "There's a fire comin', girl.

Don't you watch the news? I got batteries from Wal-Mart this morning and filled the tubs with water."

Laine hung her head. Her aunt's house—an expressive replica of a mid-nineteenth-century Victorian—was precious to her, but this had gotten out of hand. "That's hurricane preparation. Sandbags and tubs of water aren't going to help you in a fire."

"Sure they will." She looked at Steve, who'd taken a seat across from her. "Don't you fire people use sand and water to put out fires?"

Steve started to answer, but obviously caught Laine's glare and decided to bite into his burger instead.

"These fires are put out with special chemicals, from a long distance," Laine said.

Aunt Jen, who acted as though she was only half listening, frowned at her fruit salad. "Just this morning those forestry people said what they really needed to fight the fires was rain." She gestured with her fork. "Rain is water, isn't it?"

Laine looked at Steve, who suppressed a smile—the traitor—and decided she needed fat and calories for the strength to continue the fight. She sat next to Jen and dug into her hamburger, practically moaning in ecstasy when the spices and juices exploded in her mouth.

At that moment, she happened to catch Steve's eye. He'd stopped with a pineapple chunk halfway to his mouth and was staring at her.

She swallowed, recalling other meals in this kitchen where they'd stared at each other, anticipating something entirely different than whatever they were eating. Aunt Jen had usually told them stories about her bridge group and about how Delores Moleno always tried to cheat, then got insulted and left early whenever somebody called her on it.

But all Laine had wanted was the moment Jen went to bed or outside to talk to the neighbors, the moment she and Steve would be alone. She could breathe again when his hands were on her, when the heat of his body melded with hers and desire made her heart pound and her breasts tingle.

"Don't distract that boy, Laine," her aunt said abruptly. "I'm never going to get all those bags in place by myself."

"Steve has better things to do than haul sandbags around your house." He opened his mouth, presumably to deny this, so Laine rushed on, "And you're not doing it, either, Aunt Jen. All we need is to have you in the hospital with a hernia."

"My back is as strong as yours," Jen said.

"Probably so. And you can use it. We're going to pack up as many of your antiques and doll collection as we can and haul them across town to the storage facility I rented for you."

"My things will be fine right here."

Laine tossed her hands in the air, then rose to get the iced-tea pitcher from the fridge. Talking sense into that woman was like trying to get a cow to walk downstairs—which she understood was anatomically impossible. She was really beginning to think she needed to come up with a desperate plan in case her aunt refused to evacuate if the time came. She was hoping when Jen saw the billowing smoke and flames rolling toward her, she'd get wise and leave.

But she wasn't counting on it. She envisioned Jen tying herself to her Victorian-era china cabinet and refusing to budge.

What if she had to get the sheriff to arrest her and drag her away? Or maybe she'd wind up calling the doctor, who'd tranquilize her.

"Ms. Baker," Steve began in a gentle voice, "we're doing everything we can. We really hope you won't have to evacuate, but I think you should be prepared. I'll be glad to stay and help you do some packing this afternoon."

"You're not gonna charm me outta here, boy," Aunt Jen said bluntly as she pushed to her feet. "I'm a lot tougher than my niece, you know."

Tea pitcher in hand, Laine whirled toward her aunt. "He's just trying to help."

Jen tossed her wrappers—and her unfinished fruit cup—in the trash. "Yeah, yeah."

"Of course you're strong," Steve conceded way more graciously than Laine would have. "And that's how you're going to get through the next few days easily. But think of your friends, other members of your community who aren't so fortunate. They're going to need someone to lean on, someone who can stay cool in a crisis."

Aunt Jen angled her head. "Iris Wilson will probably have to be sedated."

"Someone will need to help organize the shelters and be sure the meals are being prepared."

"And watch for looters," Aunt Jen added. "Marlene Lipperman has been known to slip rolls into her purse."

I'll be damned. Laine couldn't suppress a slight smile. He was actually making progress.

Steve raised his eyebrows. "Of course. And who knows things like that besides you?" He rose and crossed to her, laying his arm around her shoulders. "Why don't you start a list of things you want us to take to storage? Laine and I will finish cleaning up in here."

"Well, if I'm gonna be working at the shelters, I'm gonna need more help than just cleaning up the kitchen."

"We'll be here for you the rest of the day," Steve said.

"Great. Let's start with my dolls."

He walked her toward the doorway. "Why don't you see if you can find your insurance papers, too. We should make sure all those dolls—"

"And my china."

"And the china are listed the way you want. Then we'll start packing."

Jen stopped just outside the door. A smile spread across her face. A smile that Laine didn't like one little bit. "My insurance papers are just fine—locked in a safety-deposit box at the bank. And as I've told my niece many times over the last few days, I am *not* packing. I am *not* leaving my home."

Steve took a step toward her. "But the dolls, the china. You said—"

"You'll be *cleaning* dolls and china today, young man." Aunt Jen whirled. "You might want to grab a duster, window cleaner and rubber gloves," she added over her shoulder as she skipped down the hall.

"She's making me crazy," Laine said, shaking her head.

Steve faced her, leaning one shoulder against the door frame. "We'll convince her."

"In the meantime, you've bought yourself endless hours of dusting. Congratulations."

"It'll give me a chance to convince you to go out with me."

"Not gonna happen," Laine said with more conviction than she felt.

"Don't you think we should talk about our relationship?"

She strode past him and out of the room. "We don't have a relationship. I've got to get something from my room," she added. "I'll be right back."

Upstairs, she brushed her teeth and dug deep for some willpower. Since he'd invited himself to hang out all afternoon, she was going to be in extended proximity to the ultimate temptation. She needed to remind herself why he was a big no-no.

She had a job to do—a job she wasn't entirely confident about or sure she'd get to keep past today. He had a fan club of women she had no intention of competing against. They lived halfway across the country from each other. His job had been, and always would be, dangerous.

Oh, and the big one—the last time they'd been together she was way more hooked on him than he was on her. She had no intention of going through that, and the resulting heartbreak, again.

"Ready to start cleaning?"

Laine poked her head out the bathroom doorway. Steve, lying on his back on the bed, waved at her.

I don't believe this.

"What do you think you're doing up here?"

"Afternoon nap?"

"Try again."

"A quick roll in the hay?"

She simply shook her head.

"We had some great times in this room." He patted the frilly white comforter. "In this bed."

Laine fought against the warmth threatening to roll through her. "Thanks for the memories," she managed to say sarcastically.

He propped himself up on his elbows. "You used to be easier than this."

"Pardon me?"

"Not like that. I mean softer. Not so tough."

"Maybe you've just lost your touch."

Bad idea. You've challenged him.

She sensed her mistake the moment the words were out of her mouth. His gaze locked with hers, he straightened, swung his legs off the bed, then rose. As he moved toward her, panic skittered through her. There was no place to retreat except into the bathroom, so she slid along the edge of the wall, praying she could escape the bedroom before he touched her.

"Remember the things we did in here?" he asked in a deep, measured voice.

She shook her head.

He smiled and kept coming.

"Look, Steve, we need to find those dusters, remember?"

"I think I remember where everything is."

"And my aunt is right down the hall—"

"Don't worry. I locked the door." He used his body to press her back against the wall. "I need you." He pinned her hands above her head. "I have to have you."

Despite her warnings and vows, her traitorous body arched into him.

He planted openmouthed kisses against the side of her neck. "You taste delicious."

She moaned.

He pressed his hips, the hardness between his legs, against her softness. "You feel even better."

Her body vibrated, her nipples tightened, as if remembering him and anticipating the pleasure he could give. It had been a while since she'd felt the soar of completion and nothing as powerful as what she'd shared with Steve.

Wasn't that why she was fighting so hard against his allure? She knew if she gave in, she might never get out.

But, boy, did she want to give in.

How many nights had she lain awake after she left California and dreamed of touching him again? And now she had him.

She slid her hands along his arms, then up his chest. Every hard, glorious inch of him.

He trailed kisses up her throat, then captured her mouth, thrusting his tongue between her lips. She gripped the top of his shoulders and closed her eyes. He gave his all to a kiss. His body, his focus. She felt surrounded by him, supported by him…consumed by him.

He yanked her shirt from her khaki pants, then ran

his hands up her stomach. The calluses on his palms reminded her of the work he did, the sacrifices he made, the bravery that was as much a part of him as his hands. He cupped her breast, rubbing his thumb across her nipple through her thin cotton bra.

As she held the back of his neck and pressed into his touch, she ached to feel the naked length of him alongside her, to hear him laugh and feel his body go rigid with pleasure.

How could she turn away from this chemistry they created? In a few days, once the fire was finally contained, she'd go home to Texas, and he'd go back to Georgia. She'd have to help her sister close down Temptation. She'd return to her humdrum small town.

But the drumming she heard at the moment was coming from the door.

"That heavy breathing I hear better be because you're washing windows, boy."

4

STEVE BANGED HIS HEAD against the wall. "She lives to do that, doesn't she?"

"I expect so."

With his heart hammering and all the strength he possessed, he released Laine and stepped back. He stared at her—at her flushed face, wide eyes and full lips. He should be running as fast as he could away from her, not inviting to torture himself with her smile or even her frown.

He'd managed to overwhelm her with their heat, but she'd come back to her senses soon. She'd remind him about her job and their past, about his fan club, about his job and their lack of compatibility.

She didn't want him here. Why was he going after her? Why couldn't he walk away? Firefighting was in his blood. He couldn't be someone he wasn't. Not even for her.

Could he?

"You look really serious all of a sudden," she said.

"I shouldn't have—"

She laid her finger over his lips. "Don't apologize. You'll spoil it."

"Laine," Aunt Jen called through the door, "do I need to get my crowbar?"

Laine didn't budge her gaze from his. "No, Aunt Jen. We'll be downstairs in a minute."

"I need help moving the doll cabinet."

"Okay," she called. Then to him, she said, "We should go help her."

He didn't move. "Yeah."

"I'd forgotten," she said softly. "I relived our time together over and over, but I'd still forgotten how it was. How…"

"Good?"

She shook her head.

He frowned. "Bad?"

She licked her lips. "Wild."

Dear God. He grabbed her hand and yanked her against him. She tucked her head beneath his chin and wrapped her arms around his waist.

"I shouldn't want you," she said.

"But you do anyway?" he asked, half joking, half hoping.

"Yes."

He tightened his grip on her. "And what are we going to do about that?"

"I have no idea."

Not exactly the answer he was looking for. The old him would have pushed and prodded, using any means he could—including her body—to get what he wanted. He wouldn't have thought past the moment he followed her down into her bed.

But he wanted more than her body this time around. He'd missed something rare and wonderful by keeping their relationship easy and casual before. The feelings rumbling around inside him were anything but casual, and until he could figure out what that meant, he expected he'd never be satisfied.

"Do you want some space?"

She leaned back, staring up at him suspiciously. "You're offering me space."

"If that's what you want."

"What's in this for you?"

He stroked her cheek. "You. Just you."

Her gaze softened for a moment, then she said, "You're trying to seduce me."

"Definitely." But there was also more.

"It's possible it's working," she said, though she stepped back, and he immediately missed her warmth. "For now we're cleaning, then I've got pictures to edit and e-mail, then go to this town hall meeting. Maybe we can have a drink afterward?"

"How about dinner?"

"That may be pushing it."

"Drinks then."

"Fine." She grabbed his hand and tugged him across the room. "Out you go. I need to change."

He leaned back against the wall next to the doorway. "I don't mind waiting."

"Cute." She flung open the door.

They found Aunt Jen standing in the hall, tapping a nasty-looking black iron crowbar against her palm.

He scooted out the door and backed down the hall. "I was just leaving."

"Just remember he's your cleaning help for the day," Laine reminded her aunt before she closed the door.

Alone with Aunt Jen in the hall, Steve decided she looked distinctly disappointed that she wouldn't be bludgeoning anyone that afternoon. "So then get into the back bedroom and move that cabinet."

Steve wasn't about to argue.

Laine appeared in the doll-collection room a few minutes later, as he handed the first, now-dusted doll to Jen for inspection. They cleaned all afternoon, barely withstanding Aunt Jen's picky requests and barking orders. Then, while Laine worked on her photos, he drove back to Josh's to shower and change, promising to pick her up at six-thirty.

"You goin' out with us tonight?" Josh asked when he walked into the kitchen to get a soda.

"No," he said as he popped open the can. "I'm going to the town hall meeting."

Josh grabbed a beer bottle. "What for?"

"Laine will be there."

"Ah." He dropped into a kitchen chair. "And how's that going?"

"I'm not sure."

Josh laughed. "Women'll make you crazy, man."

Steve really wished he could listen to that sage advice.

When he arrived at Aunt Jen's, Laine was sitting on the porch swing. She stood as he approached. "It feels like rain, don't you think?"

"I... Uh—" The sight of Laine in a silky white camisole, a tan cotton jacket and matching tan capris had rendered him speechless. The shorter-length pants allowed him a perfect view of her tan stiletto pumps, which sent his blood pressure soaring for some reason.

Maybe because he pictured her in the camisole, the shoes…and nothing else.

"The breeze—there's a certain coolness to it."

From where he stood, he felt nothing but heat. He tugged his shirt away from his body repeatedly in an effort to find this breeze she was talking about. "I'm not so sure."

"Bye, Aunt Jen," she called over her shoulder, then walked down the steps. She linked her arm through his. "Think positive."

"I am." But not necessarily about the weather. "Are those shoes…practical for working?"

"Not really. But I like them. I can always kick them off. Sometimes I do my best work barefoot."

His camisole fantasy could accommodate that. "Uh-huh." He opened the Jeep door and held her hand as she shifted her camera bag and climbed into the seat. "Either way works for me."

She looked at him over her shoulder. "Should I be reading more into that comment?"

"Of course." He slid the pad of his thumb across her bottom lip. "Have you thought any more about what we should do?"

"I haven't really had time."

"You could just go with your instincts."

"My instincts tell me to run as far away from you as possible."

"Okay, maybe not." He slid his hand down her thigh. "How about your body? What's it saying?"

"You're getting some votes there."

He'd promised her space, knowing how hard that vow would be to keep, but not realizing he'd ache to break it so quickly. "You'll let me know when the votes are all counted?"

"You'll be the first."

He stepped back, then closed the door, hoping he could get his body and his thoughts under control by the time he rounded the other side of the rented Jeep. But as he closed his own door, and the scent of her fruity perfume filled the cab, his thoughts zipped right back into forbidden-land.

Her skin was like peaches—soft, flushed. He wanted to see that flush spread all over. He wanted to lose himself in her scent and her arms.

Last night he'd only wanted to spend time with Laine to jolt himself out of his depression about Tommy's death, to remind him of times he'd been free, wild and happy. He supposed he'd accomplished that, but he'd also stepped into an unsure area, where being with her had taken on a life of its own.

Where that path would lead them, he had no idea. But he intended to see it through to the end.

As the mayor of Fairfax talked about disaster preparedness—gathering vital documents and personal valuables—and advised his citizens to consider videotaping the contents of their homes, Laine leaned against the left-side wall and clicked her camera shutter.

With their serious but sympathetic faces, Jeff Arnold and the local police chief made an especially interesting shot. She also caught images of several families, the faces of the parents lined with worry as they held the hands of their children.

Other than the reason for the meeting, the only negative aspect to the night was a minor annoyance that, in the past, would have caused her anxiety for days. Tonight, she merely shrugged.

Steve's fan club had followed him.

Since he was sitting in the front row, they had parked themselves behind him—much to the aggravation of the people around them, who were actually trying to listen to the presentation. The women giggled and flirted with Steve, then Josh and Cole, who'd been in the hall when she and Steve arrived. The guys had graciously talked to the club when Steve had ignored them. Come to think of it, maybe Josh and Cole were responsible for the fan club appearance in the first place.

As the mayor made his closing remarks, Laine caught Steve's gaze. He smiled and gave her a thumbs-up. Inwardly sighing, she returned his smile.

What the hell was she doing here with him? Besides satisfying her suddenly raging hormones.

If they spent any more time together, they were going to wind up in bed. A hot and heavy affair would ensue. For about a week.

And while she was working on conquering her fear of heights, and her libido was rapidly overruling her brain, she was terrified of falling for him. Was she crazy to go out with him? What would happen *after* drinks?

The very thought made her body vibrate. Her cautious nature was digging in its heels, even as part of her longed for risk and excitement. Given the heat she and Steve generated, was heartbreak really such a bad trade? Was prudence really stamped on her DNA?

"Thank you all for coming," the mayor said. "Good night."

Laine held back as the meeting broke up, then approached Jeff. "Thanks for inviting me. I think I got some great shots for my piece."

"Good." He turned his head, staring out over the crowd. "Now we just hope they listen."

"You're worried they won't?"

"There are always a few who think they're indestructible. Who think they can protect their property by hosing down the house with water, or by battling back the flames with a fire extinguisher and determination."

Aunt Jen to a T. And the one person who should have been listening to the warnings was in the meeting room next door organizing a potluck dinner.

Laine bit her lip. "I can't imagine," she mumbled.

They said their goodbyes, then Laine turned to find Steve.

Who was now surrounded by the fan club.

Don't these women ever give up? The man-to-woman ratio in this town must be ten to one. Though she agreed he looked delicious in black pants and a crisp white shirt, the sleeves rolled up almost to his elbows.

Standing outside the huddle, she considered the best way to disperse the giggling crowd. She could yell "fire." But they would probably just hide behind him, waiting for him to save them. She considered Steve's sister-in-law, Cara, and the gun she'd had strapped to her side the night before.

Too drastic?

She watched a tall blonde stroke Steve's arm.

Maybe not.

Thankfully, the decision was taken from her hands when Aunt Jen showed up. "Soup's on," she said, then scowled in the direction of the fan club. "Did Brad Pitt come in when I wasn't looking?"

"It's Steve."

"Well, go in there and get him, girl. The pot roast is going fast."

Laine raised her eyebrows. "You have a whistle in you?"

"Do you?"

On three, they simultaneously blew piercing whistles that probably stopped traffic in the street outside.

The entire group turned and stared in their direction. Laine bowed. Steve grinned. As Aunt Jen wished her a good evening and he walked toward her, Laine got a few nasty looks, though the crowd quickly consoled themselves with Josh and Cole.

"I guess you're ready to go?" Steve asked.

Still not sure it was a good idea to be alone with him, Laine nodded. "Sure."

"Hey, Steve," Josh called. "The ladies want to go to the Wrath. You game?"

"What's the Wrath?" Laine asked.

"An overcrowded dance club. And if you go with Josh, you usually get home around 3:00 a.m."

Owning a bar, Laine didn't go out to clubs often. When her sister was in a wild mood, she'd just invite a local band to perform and turn Temptation into one. She'd seen Cat slow dance and flirt with patrons and band members alike. Laine usually wound up as the responsible one tending bar.

Observing, not participating. Her motto.

But since she was weak, when she should probably be strong where Steve was concerned, this seemed like the perfect escape.

"We'd love to go," she said before Steve could turn down his friend, which it looked as if he was going to do.

He grabbed her hand as she started toward Josh. "I thought we were going for drinks."

She forced a smile. "We were. We are. It'll be fun. I never get to go out when I'm home."

"I thought your mom owned a bar."

"She does. Did. Actually, my sister and I have been running it the past few years since she retired. But it's closing. The city's widening the road and tossing us out. Besides, there I wind up serving drinks half the time. I want someone to wait on me." She actually tried a pleading look she'd seen dozens of women use in the bar. "Come on, Steve. Please?"

He cast a glance at Josh, then back at her. "Whatever you want."

Josh and Cole approached with a woman on each side and several more trailing behind. "So, who's driving?"

"I can," Steve said, though he didn't look thrilled about it.

Laine could relate. The few times she did go out she usually got stuck being the designated driver. She started to tell Steve she'd changed her mind. She could go over the shots she'd taken during the meeting, though her editor actually seemed pleased with the ones she'd sent earlier.

"But my Jeep holds five—tops," Steve went on.

Josh and Cole obviously had no intention of giving up any of the girls, so they dug into their pockets for cab fare.

TWO HOURS LATER, as music and lights pulsed around her, Laine couldn't decide if the floor was actually jumping beneath her feet or if the pounding in her head had penetrated her entire body.

Not that she'd ever had much of a wild youth, but she was quite certain going out on the town had changed drastically in the last few years. Music was more chanting than singing. Dancing was more of a bumping-and-grinding, sex-simulation thing. And it was the women, not the men, you had to fend off kisses from.

As yet another woman lay back on the table in front of her, Laine scooted back her chair. People didn't do regular shots. They did body shots, which involved someone pouring a shot of liquor on a woman's stomach, then a guy would slurp the liquid from her navel.

She really wished she'd packed some Wet Wipes in her purse, 'cause these women were going to need them later.

"I guess those belly-baring shirts come in handy sometimes," she yelled in Steve's ear.

Yelling was another drawback to clubbing. She wasn't going to have a voice in the morning.

Steve angled his head as Cole valiantly licked liquor off the laughing woman's body. "Wanna give it a try?"

Laine shook her head. She'd done a couple of regular shots after Josh challenged her, so she felt tingly and out-of-body-like, but she wasn't that far gone. The whole business could be fun in private, she supposed, but in the middle of a bar, with dozens of people looking on? No way. Adventure she was trying to embrace. Hedonism was something else entirely.

If only she was doing a pictorial on *Girls Gone Wild*…

Suddenly Josh jerked her out of her chair. "Come dance with me, Laine."

"I really—"

"Oh, come on. Steve's cool with it."

She had one last glimpse of Steve's frowning—and not looking at all "cool with it"—face before Josh dragged her through the crowd and onto the packed floor. He pulled her into his arms in a more traditional dance rather than the humping moves of most everyone else, for which she was grateful. She also noticed he smelled good—spicy and manly. He had a good body. A nice smile. A mischievous personality.

She waited for the desire that always slid through her body whenever Steve touched her, but nothing happened.

His hand was warm and confident in hers, but she didn't vibrate. She didn't imagine his hands gliding across her skin, then his lips following the same path. She didn't want to clutch him against her, rub her palms over his chest, explore his body and make his muscles twitch.

Well, that sucked.

"Our boy Steve is really tied up in knots over you," he said loudly in her ear.

She leaned back and met his gaze. "He is?"

"Yep."

"And that's a bad thing?"

He shrugged. "I guess not."

"Then why'd you bring it up?"

At first she didn't think he was going to answer, then he finally admitted, "Tommy's death really screwed with him. I just don't want to see him hurt any more."

"And you think I could hurt him?"

"Yep."

While she was digesting this unbelievable bit of information, he went on. "If you're not interested in him, you need to say so. Don't string him along."

"I'm not."

"If you say so."

As they continued to dance, she blocked out the crowd and the pounding music in an effort to be honest with herself, to see herself from another side. Maybe she *was* stringing him along, though not for the reasons Josh obviously thought—that she was the kind of woman who enjoyed teasing.

Though she *had* suggested drinks with him then grabbed the chance to bring along Josh and the others because she was concerned about getting hurt herself. She also felt weirdly empowered by the idea that she might be able to hurt him.

Of course, Josh might be full of bull, too.

The deejay blessedly played an R & B ballad, allowing her to consider her plan. She owed it to herself and Steve to make a decision. Did she want a wild fling? Did she want to continue to see Steve? Did—

"My turn, Josh."

She turned to find herself face-to-face with the man himself. His blue eyes were dark. With determination? Anger? Maybe even jealousy? He held out his hand, and she took it without hesitation.

In his arms, longing washed over her. The chemistry missing with Josh roared to life with Steve. She breathed deeply of his scent and slid her fingers through the hair at his nape. He felt so strong and perfect.

She wanted him like crazy.

As they moved in tandem and their hips brushed, she clutched him tighter. How could she walk away from something as powerful as this? Was she kidding herself that she could work in this town every day and not want to be with him? Could she commit her body to him, knowing her heart wouldn't allow her to fall for him and accept the dangerous, if heroic, job he did?

Suddenly a commotion erupted a few feet over, and Laine turned her head, frowning at the interruption until she heard a panicked voice shout, "Someone get a doctor!"

Before she even blinked, Steve was rushing over. She followed, and when she reached the cluster of people near the center of the dance floor, she found Steve kneeling next to a young woman who was flat on her back and twitching uncontrollably.

"Does anyone know her?" he called out.

Several people shook their heads and glanced at each other. Laine dropped to her knees on the other side of the girl. She was pale, and when Laine laid her hand on her arm in an effort to still her seizure, she found her skin cold and clammy.

Even as panic started to race over her, she swallowed and ordered herself to calm down. Steve was in control. He was a paramedic as well as a firefighter.

He tossed her his cell phone. "Call 911. Tell them you need medics—an unexplained seizure."

Hands shaking, Laine did as he asked while he tilted the girl's head back and peered inside her mouth. "Airway clear." Then he grabbed her hand. A silver Medic Alert bracelet was wrapped around her wrist. "She's diabetic. Pulse racing. Hypoglycemia. She probably drank too much." He rolled her to her left side. "She needs oxygen and glucose."

Laine repeated everything he said into the phone and was told a unit was just a few blocks away and would be there within moments.

"How much did she drink? Did anybody see?" Steve called, glancing up at the crowd.

A thin, blond-headed girl shuffled forward after encouragement by the girls behind her. "I saw her down three shots of Jack Daniel's."

"When was the last time she ate anything?"

"I'm not sure. We hooked up here about an hour ago."

Three shots of JD in an hour? Laine knew *she'd* be unconscious. She couldn't imagine what that might do to a diabetic on an empty stomach.

"Anybody got a jacket?" Steve called.

A guy in the crowd stripped off his jean jacket and tossed it at Steve. He placed it beneath the girl's head, then held her shoulders steady, no doubt in an effort to keep her from hurting herself. Laine shoved the phone in her back pocket and tried to comfort the girl.

The odd twitching seemed to go on forever, punctuated by the sudden silence as the deejay cut the music. Buzzing voices filled the void. Oppressive heat filled the room. The manager appeared, then Josh, asking if they could help. Steve suggested Josh wait at the door for the medics.

As he ran off, Laine's gaze unexpectedly caught Steve's. The controlled intensity she saw sent a kick of reassurance through her, much different than the unquenched hunger they'd shared moments ago, but still just as powerful.

In the distance sirens wailed, and she looked away. *He really is a hero.*

Once the paramedics came and went, taking their now-stable patient with them, Steve got a standing ovation from the bar. The deejay dedicated a song to him. He even found some songs that featured the whine of an electric guitar and a few lyrics Laine understood. The women, naturally, gathered around him in a giggling circle.

By the time they reached their table, everyone, not just Laine, realized how special he was. They all wanted to buy him a drink, but since he was the designated driver, they collected in front of her. Between toasting him and eating the fiery buffalo wings somebody ordered, she wound up drinking way more than she should have. Before she knew it, she was gazing at him like a starry-eyed teen and not really sure she could stand and hold steady at the same time.

"I think you're drunk," he said as she trailed her hand through the hair just above his ear.

"No. Just really…" She grinned. "Loose."

His eyes lit. "We could go. Josh and Cole can get a cab home."

"I'm afraid to be alone with you right now," she admitted with a truthfulness that could only come after midnight.

"Why?"

She cupped his cheek. "'Cause I want you too much."

"I'm not really sure how that's a problem."

"I'm just leery, I guess." She paused. "After last time."

"We're different people now. Maybe things will be different."

His body heat seemed to surround her, pulling her closer, reminding her of intimacies they'd shared. "I felt a distinct emotional deficit last time."

"You— What?"

"I was more into you than you were into me."

"Ah." He leaned closer, his breath brushing her face. "I don't agree with that. But I *was* young. And selfish. And I should have talked to you about your reservations with my job. I shouldn't have enjoyed my popularity so much."

"Popularity?"

"The fan club phenomenon."

She smiled. "So you admit you have one?"

"No. But I get what you're saying. I enjoyed attention that made you feel insecure. I should have tuned in to it."

"I'm not insecure about it anymore."

"No?"

"No. I've decided to accept your popularity as a sign of my good taste."

"That still seems pretty flattering in my favor. How about my job?"

"I'm still struggling."

"Did I mention the cats I save from trees?"

"I think you did. But that's not the highlight of your day."

A shadow fell over his eyes briefly, then he smiled. "Not exactly."

The risk of his job and her heart was something she had to consider carefully if she thought they had any chance of a future. But, for now, she was content just to be with him. For now, she wasn't thinking about anything but the moment.

He slid his lips across her cheek. "I still think our chemistry should override your hesitation."

"Maybe that's just because you're tied up in knots over me."

He leaned back, his eyes sparkling with laughter. "Am I?"

"Josh said you were. Is it true?"

"Maybe."

She pursed her lips.

"Okay, so maybe I shouldn't have let you go so easily before. And now…"

Laine sucked in a breath, then released it. "Now?"

"I don't intend to make the same mistake twice."

"And after the danger of the fire passes?"

His gaze searched hers, and in it she saw the same confusion and desire she'd felt every moment since she'd seen him again. "I have no idea."

"If you two get any closer," Josh said as he leaned between them, "you're gonna have to do a lap dance."

She and Steve didn't bother to turn their heads, but simultaneously said, "Not going to happen."

"Go away," Steve added.

"How about Laine doing a body shot?"

"Forget it," she said.

"Our big hero at least deserves a kiss."

Laine glanced at Josh, who was at his best when he was causing trouble, then back to Steve. He *was* the big hero of the night. And infinitely kissable.

What the hell!

She grabbed the lapels of his shirt, pulled him to her and kissed him long and deep.

After that, though she still didn't participate, she got into the spirit of the body shots. Maybe because Steve was tucked comfortably by her side. Maybe because she was grateful to be alive. Maybe it was the unrelenting, pulsing music, or the crowd's party-till-dawn attitude. A lot of people were no doubt releasing tension related to the impending fire.

The wildfire was raging through the outlying areas, and central Fairfax was next. If guys like Steve, Josh and Cole couldn't battle back the blaze, Laine didn't hold out much hope for anybody else.

5

STEVE GLANCED at his unconscious passenger. He'd been hoping, despite her reservations about getting involved with him again, that the night was going to end with them finally giving in to their carnal urges. He firmly believed they could work out most of their differences in bed.

They were both going to bed soon, he supposed, just not the same one, and definitely not participating in the activity he'd planned. And with Josh going home with someone, they would have had the apartment to themselves.

Shaking his head in regret, he pulled into Aunt Jen's driveway. After he scooped Laine into his arms, he carried her up the porch steps. She mumbled something incoherent, then buried her face against his neck.

The woman was going to be the death of him.

And, as he glanced at the hairnet and bathrobe-clad figure standing in the doorway, he realized he might not even die from need. He could meet his end via a crowbar and lots of senior-citizen attitude.

"Evening, Ms. Baker," he said cautiously, keeping a close watch on the crowbar she was tapping against her palm.

"What'd you do to my niece?" she asked in a harsh whisper, glaring at him.

"She fell asleep. I was just going to carry her to her room."

"Uh-huh. This is a Christian household, Mr. Kimball. I don't allow unmarried guests of the opposite sex to share rooms."

"I'm not staying."

"You better believe you're not." She opened the screen door, then stepped back. "Straight to her room. And remember, I'm right behind you."

How could I forget?

Steve shifted Laine's weight and proceeded down the hall and up the stairs. The moonlight streaming through the window in her room allowed him to see well enough to lay her on the bed. He started to pull back the comforter and sheets, but figured he'd pushed his luck enough with Aunt Jen.

She leaned around him. "She smells like whiskey." She wrinkled her nose. "And smoke. Where the devil have you two been?"

"At a club in—"

She waved her hand. "Never mind. I don't want to know." She pointed toward the door with the crowbar. "Out."

"Can I kiss her first?"

"Absolutely not. She's unconscious."

He'd had an entire clubful of people in the palm of his hand for hours. Why couldn't he manage one small elderly woman? "Will you at least tell her I'll call her tomorrow?"

She narrowed her eyes, as if searching for something suspicious in that statement, then finally nodded.

As he turned to go, he decided he needed to make Aunt Jen liking him a major priority. If Laine sat around all the time listening to her aunt's lousy opinion of him, he'd likely be barred from the property by the end of the week.

So, when he arrived the next morning to see Laine, he brought coffee and doughnuts for three.

"You should have taken me up on dinner," he said when she appeared at the front door.

Wearing a wrinkled, overlarge orange T-shirt and sunglasses, she held an ice pack to her head. "Don't talk so loud."

He fought back a smile. There were advantages to being the designated driver. "You could have had a nice *quiet* dinner last night, remember? It was your big idea to trade that for wings and whiskey."

She leaned against the door frame. "I'm not even sure if it was the food, the alcohol or the music that did it to me."

"Probably a combination of all three. How about some coffee?"

Straightening, she dropped the ice pack. "Coffee? You brought coffee? Why didn't you say so in the first place?" She snatched a cup from the drinks carrier, sipped, then sighed as if he'd done something much more pleasurable than hand her a beverage. "I may live after all."

"I brought enough for Aunt Jen, too."

"She's not here. She went to the church to organize meals for the evacuees."

He fought the urge to applaud. Maybe his good deed from last night had been rewarded. He walked with Laine into the kitchen, setting the doughnut box on the table and sitting next to her.

"Have you heard anything about the weather?" she asked after another bracing sip of coffee.

"Just what was on the morning news, and that doesn't look good. I'll know more when I get to base camp later today."

She took her time selecting a doughnut, finally deciding on a chocolate-covered one. "You're working later?"

She asked casually, as if they were talking about him strolling to his office downtown. He wished she'd take off the sunglasses so he could see her eyes. His job was a major point of contention between them. He wanted to press her about her reservations, but wouldn't broaching the subject force him to be honest with her about smoke jumping? That he dreaded every moment of the whole ordeal. And after she'd led the toast of "our hero" to him last night over and over, he already felt like a fraud.

Everybody else on the team wanted to conquer the fire that had taken Tommy's life. Steve didn't see the point in raging at an act of nature. Nothing would bring back Tommy.

"I'm going out with a hotshot crew later," he said finally, hoping she wouldn't press. Pretending enthusiasm for his job was starting to feel like lying.

"Oh." Thankfully she dropped the subject. "After I check in with my editor, I'll probably go up there, too. Or help Aunt Jen at the shelters."

He rose and tossed his empty cup in the trash. "We're not doing much more. Just delaying the inevitable."

"But the delay helps, right? Every hour we can hold out in hope of rain is priceless."

"I guess." When he returned to his seat, he scooted his chair closer. "I never got a kiss good-night."

She licked her lips, and he longed to lean forward and capture them with his mouth. "Did you undress me and tuck me in bed?"

"With Aunt Jen and her crowbar hovering nearby? No way."

"I really need to hide that thing."

"That would be helpful, yes."

"I'm sorry I passed out on you."

He pulled her sunglasses off and laid them on the table. "But you'll make it up to me tonight."

She placed her hands on top of his shoulders. "I'll go to dinner with you. The good-night kiss will be negotiated afterward."

He kissed her mouth lightly, then slid his lips along her cheek, where he paused. "Laine, you smell like smoke."

She shoved at his chest. "I haven't showered yet. Now, out you go, so I can get ready."

He rose, grabbing her hand and pulling her into his arms. He could get used to the smoke. "I'll be glad to wash your back."

"Shameless, that's what you are."

"And brave," he added. "What if Aunt Jen came home and caught us?"

"The doughnuts would have distracted her for a few minutes."

"I'll remember that when I climb up the rose trellis to get into your room."

"Somehow, I don't think you should try that again."

He backed her up, trapping her against the refrigerator. "But I'm a big, bad, dangerous firefighter, remember? Climbing trellises is required, according to the handbook." He placed a lingering kiss just below her ear, smiling when her breathing quickened.

"What else— Oh my, that feels good. What else is in the...handbook?"

He pressed his knee between her legs, and she gasped, wrapping her hands around his biceps. "Chapter two is particularly entertaining." He cupped her breast. "And I know you're dying to hear chapter three."

"Oh, yeah."

Though it nearly killed him, he stepped away from her. "Then you'd better get some studying in before dinner."

Openmouthed and panting, she stared at him. "What are you doing?"

"Making sure you're looking forward to tonight. Josh and the others won't be there to save you." He rubbed his thumb across her bottom lip. "To protect you from yourself."

She planted her hands on her hips and pointed toward the doorway. "Out."

"I've been thrown out of this house twice in the last twelve hours. That's gotta be some kind of record." Still, he scooted out of the kitchen as requested. Last night he'd promised her the time and space she needed, but that didn't mean he had to fight fair.

He jogged down the porch steps, then turned at the bottom to find her hovering at the front door. "Think about what you want from me, Laine. Because I *am* tied up in knots over you, and I'm not holding back this time."

"I JUST DON'T WANT to get hurt again."

"Oh, please, Laine," Denise said with a dramatic roll of her eyes. "Listen to yourself. You sound like an old woman. Take a chance. Maybe there's something more between you and Steve than just a temporary fling."

"Temporary or not," Cara said, "you're the best Steve has hooked up with since I've known him."

Laine had met Denise for lunch and found Cara eating just two booths away. They'd banded together, though she was pretty sure Steve's sister-in-law wasn't entirely comfortable with Laine's waffling about Steve. Cara seemed frustrated by Laine's inability to decide.

"Just sleep with him," Cara continued. "Get it over with."

"Get it over with?" Denise said incredulously, tucking a strand of curly red hair behind her ear.

Cara pointed her fry at Laine. "You know what I mean. Jump in. Go for it. Quit obsessing."

Laine gestured with her salad fork. "Did I mention that man got me all...*worked* up, then left?"

"He's using your body against you," Denise said. "Smart man."

"Are you on my side or his?"

Denise sipped her tea. "I'm on the side of love."

"I'm on the side of making a decision—one way or the other," Cara said. "Though a woman holding out might be a novel experience for Steve."

"You're a big help," Laine said to Cara. "I'd just gotten past the fan club thing. And this isn't love," she added to Denise.

"How do you know?"

It *couldn't* be love. Then she'd really be in trouble.

She'd stopped for lunch after spending the morning being ordered around by Aunt Jen and her friends, who all apparently thought they were the next Julia Child. Laine was hoping for a little friendly support and commiseration over Steve, his dirty tactics and her troubled feelings. Denise—and now Cara—were supposed to tell her men were all jerks and certainly not worth the trouble, and suggest they go buy shoes or chocolate.

She was so desperate for guidance, she'd even considered calling her sister, but set down the phone after running through what she planned to say. *Hi, Cat. I know I've been a complete witch nagging you, but now I need help in an area you actually know something about.* That little speech just didn't say family love and devotion.

"You said you didn't feel comfortable with your relationship before because you were more committed than he was," Denise continued in that same practical tone. "It sounds to me like that's all changed."

"It was more than that. The smoke jumping—"

"Which he's given up," Cara put in. "The Baxter Fire Department doesn't get quite as much action."

"Except when there's an arsonist running loose," Laine said.

Cara shrugged. "You've got a point there."

"And he sure came racing down here pretty fast when they asked him to." She leaned forward to make her point. She was really annoyed that the other women were making so much sense. "We also live halfway across the country from one another."

Denise sighed. "So you'll move. Or he'll move."

"But—"

"And if things don't work out between you," Denise rolled on, "then you've had some fun, rekindled an old flame you've never forgotten." She scooped up a bit of salad. "I don't see how you can lose."

Laine cast a desperate glance at Cara, who nodded in agreement with Denise. "But it's not that simple."

"I bet you drive him crazy with that stubbornness," Denise said.

Laine laid down her fork with a snap. "I do not."

Denise patted her hand. "You know I love you, girl, but you're thinking about this too much. I want you to be happy, to grab life with both hands. When we got here, you spent fifteen minutes deciding what you wanted off a six-item menu. If you make the wrong decision, you fix it." She shrugged. "Or you learn. And you *move on.*

"And think about this—with the bar closing you have nothing holding you to Texas. You won't be abandoning your sister or your mother or your responsibilities by taking your own chance on happiness."

Even as Laine listened to all this, she still doubted. "I'm not really good at risk. I'm doing my job for the money. I've spent years photographing flowers and getting my sister out of trouble."

"I don't see that," Cara said. "I see a woman who knows what she wants, who's not afraid to go after it. And, hey, if he screws up, remind him that I'm armed. I'll be there for you."

"And I promise to catch you if you fall." Denise smiled. "Or at least buy you a big tub of ice cream."

STEVE HACKED AWAY the tree branch, then tossed it to Josh, who was just behind him. "Ready for a beer?"

"Been ready," Josh said. "See if Cole's got any in his thermos."

Knowing he was kidding, Steve still called out to Cole, "Hey, man, got a Bud on you?"

Moving through the brush just a few feet away, Cole said, "Oh, yeah. Got a six-pack in the first-aid kit."

"I think we should have the chief drop a keg down here, rather than water," Josh added.

"Just give me a straw," Cole said.

"A straw?" Josh asked. "I'm not drinkin' out of no damn straw."

Steve hacked at another branch. "I guess you're just gonna open the keg and stick your whole head in."

"Damn straight," Josh said.

They'd spent most of the day digging a trench around the hot-spot fire that had popped up a couple of miles from the main blaze. At least with the arrival of reinforcements that morning, they were all able to work shorter shifts. In light of Tommy's death, Chief Arnold wasn't taking any chances on safety.

Heat from the fire burning less than a hundred yards away had sweat rolling down Steve's face and back, but he pressed on. There was no other choice.

As he had every day he'd been working the fire, he ignored the past that tried to intrude. He closed out the vision of the charred trees and suffocating smoke that had dominated the landscape of the Cleveland National Forest. He pretended he didn't see his partner's bleeding arm, cut by a slip of the hacksaw when they'd both fallen down a ridge that had collapsed under their feet. He fought against the old pain from his own leg, broken in two places. He ignored the crushing feeling in his chest, the one that reminded him so vividly of the endless hours he'd spent inside a small cave, trapped by the fire and wondering if he'd ever see the north Georgia mountains and his family again.

There was so much he'd loved about smoke jumping—the exhilaration, the adventure, the realization that you were doing a job very few were willing to sign up for, the camaraderie with his jump team. But the intense pressure in his chest, the sensation he felt every time he descended into the woods, reminded him that he shouldn't be here.

Fear of his memories held him back; fear of his friends discovering his secret kept him moving forward.

He ground to a halt as he and Josh reached a clearing. The site before him effectively pushed the nightmares of the past away.

A token effort had been made to clean up and disguise the scene, but Steve knew he was looking at an abandoned campsite.

"What's up?" Josh asked, stepping around him. "Who the hell's been out here?"

Thinking of Cara's mission, the site immediately took on a suspicious slant. "Good question."

"It's probably old."

"Probably." Still, he knelt by the small circle that had been a fire pit and picked up a stray rock. "It's warm. Too warm."

Josh joined him, picking up a rock for himself. Behind his blast shield, his eyes widened. "What kind of idiot leaves a warm campfire in the middle of a forest fire?"

"An idiot." He paused. "Or someone who just doesn't care if the fire spreads."

"You don't think that nonsense about arson is true."

"Could be." He looked around for other evidence and saw several deep, round holes that could have been made by tent stakes. "We need to tell Cara."

"Yeah." He rose, glaring down at the pit. "For this guy's sake, I hope he's just stupid."

Steve scooped up his hatchet, belying his suppressed rage and sense of injustice for Tommy. He heard the soft, almost delicate crackling of flames in the distance. He'd lied to himself earlier about not wanting to get back at an act of nature. Fires were living, breathing entities, feeding off oxygen, raging and strengthening the longer they were given what they needed. Though you knew you were never alone in the battle, every firefighter at some point faced those flames and wondered if he'd be consumed in a flash.

He didn't fear the fire, but he'd lost the drive for the unique battle that forest fires presented. And standing beside men and women who relished the challenge, who lived for the fight, was making a mockery of everything he'd vowed to defend.

Shaking away his thoughts, he noted the site's location on his global positioning tracker, then turned and followed Josh back to their trail, where they hooked up with Cole.

"Michaels to Kimball," his communicator suddenly buzzed.

"Kimball here."

"Let's call a chopper with a splash. I think we can get this one today."

"Do it." Though Michaels had more experience than Steve, the younger man always deferred to him when making decisions. Former leadership had its privileges, he supposed, though the respect made him feel awkward. "Meet at the safety zone ASAP."

Steve, Josh and Cole gathered the cut branches, then jogged west, meeting up with the rest of the team on a ridge just above the fire. By cutting off the supply of fuel with the trench and clearing stray branches, they'd contained the blaze and choked out most of its strength.

As the helicopter blades cut through the air, they all looked up. The bird hovered over the fire, then the communicator crackled. "Three, two, one…"

Water sloshed from the base of the helicopter, as if someone had just cut a hole in a rain cloud. As smoke and steam billowed up, Steve and the others high-fived. After trudging through heat and smoke all afternoon, water was a blessing.

"You've got three hours of daylight," the spotter said through the communicator. "Good luck, boys." He and the pilot saluted, then the chopper lifted and banked over the trees.

The brief break over, the team spent the time going over the site, making sure the ground was cooling, putting out any smoldering spots with the chemical tanks on their backs. By the time the sun began to set, they'd collapsed on the ground to watch the sky streak with color while Michaels informed base camp that they were ready to come home.

Steve reflected on the dozens of times he'd shared the same end of a hard day with Tommy. His friend would never see another sunset thanks to this fire. Steve couldn't reconcile himself with the anger and injustice of that.

"Cara's going to be pissed you didn't call her right away," Josh noted after a long drink from his canteen. "Now she won't be able to inspect the camp until tomorrow."

"I was a little busy."

"Still, I don't want to be around when you tell her," Josh said.

"If we catch some guy settin' these fires, Cara won't likely ever see him alive," Cole said, his face blank of its usual amenable expression.

On the flight back to base camp, Steve considered leaving Cara a message to call him tomorrow and avoiding her altogether. The woman had a habit of carrying a loaded nine-millimeter pistol wherever she went, and he wanted all his body parts intact for his date with Laine.

"You sure I can't talk you into coming out with us again?" Josh asked as the chopper touched down.

"Nope."

Cole nudged him. "Vivian's been asking about you."

"Yeah?" Steve couldn't have cared less; he couldn't even conjure up an image of Vivian. But he feigned interest. Because he didn't want to admit to his buddies how focused he was on Laine? Or because he didn't want to admit it to himself?

Neither idea was a good sign.

"Maybe another time," he said. "Don't wait up, Josh." He stepped out the open door and headed to the storage tent to stow his gear. Then he made the mistake of stopping by the command tent to make sure he was still off tomorrow.

And groaned aloud when he saw the woman typing on a laptop as she sat behind Chief Arnold's desk.

Cara merely raised her eyebrows at his rudeness. "I heard you had a good afternoon."

"Yeah." He sighed at the inevitable. "Josh and I found something that might interest you."

She stopped typing. "Really?"

He glanced at his watch. "Can we talk about this on the way to my Jeep? I'm running late."

"A date with Laine?"

"Yeah."

"We can't let a little matter like arson stand in the way of true love, now, can we?" Despite her sarcasm, she rose and snagged a black windbreaker off the back of the chair.

Steve stared at her shoulder holster before she covered it up by putting on the jacket, and decided he was taking a bigger risk with her than he had all afternoon.

"Spill it," she ordered as they exited the tent.

"We found an abandoned campsite. A recent one. The rocks around the fire pit were still warm."

She didn't move, didn't start in surprise, just mumbled, "Interesting. Specifics?"

"Some burned matches, trampled brush, holes from tent stakes. Some attempt had been made to hide it, but not much."

"Where?"

"Near the hot-spot fire we worked today." He rattled off the coordinates.

"When?"

He actually considered lying, then decided he was being ridiculous. Cara wasn't going to shoot him. "A few hours ago."

She stopped. "*Hours?* You waited *hours* to tell me?"

"I was a little busy," he said defensively, though the argument was much weaker than it had been with Josh.

Muttering, she turned her back on him. Then she whirled back, planted her hands on her hips, and he caught another glimpse of her pistol.

Hopefully, she wouldn't shoot him.

"Let's go now," she said.

He shook his head. "The chief won't let you go out there in the dark. The site will still be there tomorrow, Cara."

She pointed in the distance. "Unless the coastal winds kick up and spread my evidence halfway to L.A."

"I'm sorry. We really were pushed for time. I'll take you out there myself. With the extra help, we're only having to work every other day."

She glared at him, her blue-green eyes stormy as a hurricane. "Fine—8:00 a.m."

Steve pictured Laine...soft, warm and naked in his bed. The way he anticipated the night ending. "Ah, hell, Cara—"

"You wanna go for seven?"

"Eight's fine."

She turned away. "What's with the men in this family? They act like the sun rises at ten-thirty."

He might be pushing his luck, but he had to ask, "I don't get the camp. If an arsonist is responsible, why would he set a fire then hang out to watch it burn?"

She angled her head. "After our case last fall, I'm surprised you don't know."

"He gets off on the danger?"

"And the publicity."

"But the papers yesterday were full of news about the evacuations not the arson."

"For how much longer? Maybe he's going to give them something more to work with." She paused. "By the way, is there room to set a helicopter down nearby? I'm not much on parachuting."

"There's room." He started to tease her about her reluctance for jumping, but since he wasn't wild about it himself, he didn't push his luck or her temper further. "See ya in the morning, Captain."

"Just make sure you're—" She shook her head. "Damn. Have fun tonight."

Dirty, hot and tired, Steve still smiled. "I intend to."

HER HEART POUNDING with nerves, Laine braced her new black-patent stiletto against the running board on Steve's Jeep and climbed inside.

Take a chance, Denise had said. *Just sleep with him,* Cara had advised.

Okay. Sure. What the hell.

Thanks to a terse e-mail about close-ups of the blaze from her editor, she'd spent most of the day at the site of the main fire. She'd sweated—and not just from the heat—but she'd survived the ordeal and had some nice shots to show for her sacrifice.

Afterward she'd hoped to have some time to shop for something with a little more punch than jeans or khakis. Something on sale, preferably. Instead, she'd found a brand-new slinky black dress, matching shoes and lingerie—courtesy of Denise—sitting on Aunt Jen's front porch.

As she dressed, she reminded herself this was only about her and Steve's chemistry. She wasn't going to let her emotions take over again. She wasn't going to worry about his job, the dangers of him facing the fire. She wasn't thinking about any future past tonight. Quite a feat for a woman who organized her canned goods alphabetically. And by size. And label color.

Her libido had won her over in the voting on Steve, but she had no intention of polling her heart on the matter.

"You look beautiful," he said as he settled behind the wheel.

She looked just on the edge of trampy, but appropriate for her carnal goal. "Thanks." She let her gaze roam down his body, encased in a baby-blue shirt and dark slacks. "You're still in one piece, I see."

"Why wouldn't I be?"

"A local reporter had footage of the fire on the evening news. I assume that was you dangling from a helicopter."

"Nope. I climbed in and out of the chopper while it was on the ground." He grinned. "Just like you, I expect."

"Oh, well…good." Why was she so determined to cast him in a bad light?

You're protecting yourself, remember?

"Are you going to tell me what's in the basket now?"

She patted the bundle on her lap. "Dinner. I thought we'd drive up to the Hill."

He stared at her. "You mean *Makeout* Hill?"

"That's the one."

"Is that an invitation?"

"Where else are we going to go for privacy? You're staying at Josh's, and I have Aunt Jen the Crowbar Chaperon as a roommate."

He started the engine. "As long as you keep your hands to yourself. I think you have designs on my body."

She grinned, sliding her finger along his jaw. "I might."

Connecting with her gaze, his eyes intensely blue,

he was ready for more than just food. "Then I vote we skip dinner and go straight for dessert."

"That's because you've never tasted Aunt Jen's fried chicken."

6

ON THE DRIVE OVER they talked about mutual old friends, the amazing support from the community in Fairfax and the weather report that predicted a significant chance of rain later in the week. For the first time, Laine felt as if they were inching beyond the past, forging a new connection without dragging along as much old baggage.

When they pulled onto the Hill, the area was deserted. Since it was a Tuesday night, Laine wasn't surprised, but grateful. When things got steamy later—which she hoped they would—she didn't really feel the need for an audience.

They unpacked the basket she'd filled with chicken, pasta salad, grapes and cheese. She'd opted for a pinot grigio at the shaky recommendation of the guy at the liquor store, who wasn't all that confident about cold fried chicken and wine pairings.

She also popped a CD of country ballads into the stereo, reminding them that though they were in the foreign land of California, they had Southern roots in common. After the wild thumping beats from the bar the night before, the acoustic guitar, mandolin and piano sent warmth flowing through her veins.

Her half-full plastic wineglass dangling from her fingers, Laine leaned her seat back with a sigh. Since her other hand was linked with Steve's, and he'd opened the top of the Jeep, she felt pretty relaxed and steady about the decisions she'd made that day.

"You don't have much hope of saving the town, do you?" she asked.

He hesitated. "No. The fire's too big. We're pissin' in the wind."

"The Steve I remember would never give up."

"I haven't given up."

"Haven't you?" She turned her head, surprised to find his eyes so full of emotion. It seemed the only time he was full of life was when he looked at her. Not that she was complaining, but she also worried about him.

He was different, to be sure. More focused on her than on his friends. More mature and patient. Less reckless. But some of the changes in him seemed out of step. Forced. Wrong.

He bowed his head. "Dammit, Laine, you don't understand."

Just the opening she'd been looking for. "So tell me."

"We're givin' everything we've got. We put out small fires here and there, but no matter what we do, the fire creeps closer to Fairfax."

"And how do you feel about that?"

He narrowed his eyes. "I don't need psychoanalyzing."

She shrugged. "Who else are you going to talk to?"

He tapped his fingers against the steering wheel. "It's hard. Being out there every day. Digging and chopping and dousing the flames. I feel like an ant battling a lawn mower." His voice lowered. "We need more. Tommy deserved more."

"How would things be different if Tommy was there?"

"Easier."

"Easier how?"

"I don't know. Just easier."

"None of this is your fault, Steve."

"I know."

"Do you?"

Turning toward her, he braced his hand on the dashboard. "I'm not trying to bring Tommy back. I just—" He stopped on a sigh. "I just want to make him proud."

"You are. You're going on when he can't."

"Yeah."

Though he still didn't look happy, she thought she'd made her point. She sipped her wine. "And what about the arson? Has Cara found out anything?"

"Actually, I found something. I'm going out with her tomorrow to investigate a recently abandoned campsite."

"Weren't you putting out a hot spot today?"

"Yeah."

"Was there evidence of a fire at this campsite?"

"Oh, yeah."

She sat up straight, setting her wineglass on the floorboard. "The arsonist?"

"Could be."

"Mind if I tag along tomorrow?"

"Cara's in charge. You'll have to ask her." He studied her face. "You'll have to go in a chopper, you know."

"I've been in more choppers in the last few days than I have in my nearly thirty years of life. Not exactly my cup of tea, but I'm managing."

"It might be dangerous."

She angled her head, unsure if he was serious or not. "How?"

"It's a wildfire. Unpredictable. And, well…wild."

She leaned toward him, sliding her fingers through his hair. "Will you be there to protect me?"

He caught her hand and stilled her movements. "Yes."

He's serious. And she wasn't quite sure how their lighthearted picnic had turned into I'll Analyze You, You Analyze Me.

You started it.

"That's my job," he continued. "But I'm also thinking it's interesting how your job can be important enough for you to risk your safety."

She tried to tug her hand back, but he wouldn't let go. "I'm not risking my safety."

"You're certainly doing something you're not comfortable with."

"That's because my editor's making me."

"I've done things I'm not comfortable with, you know."

Fearless, daredevil Steve afraid of something? As if she really believed that. She did realize, however, that he was basically calling her a hypocrite for protesting the dangers of his job, when she took risks of her own.

She didn't want to argue about jobs, or the past, or the choices they'd made, but she did feel she owed him an explanation. "Look, I was tired of being cautious and shy. After we broke up, I made some changes in my life, in the way I dealt with people, the way I looked at myself. I took this job for the pay raise, but it's also part of my journey to be more assertive and confident."

"You certainly succeeded."

"Thanks." She paused, searching his gaze, reflecting on the admiration and desire in his voice. "That was a compliment, wasn't it?"

"You bet." The tension dispelled, and he spread open her hand and kissed her palm. "How assertive are we talking about?"

She lifted herself out of her seat, hiked her dress up her thighs, then swung her leg over his lap and straddled him.

Eyes wide, he braced his hands on either side of her hips. "That's pretty assertive."

She grinned. "When you want something…" She traced his bottom lip with her finger. "Or someone…"

He slid his hands up her sides, then cupped her breasts, his thumbs stroking but not quite reaching her nipples. "I don't want our first time to be in the car," he said without much conviction.

Leaning down, she tongued his earlobe. Memories from the past washed over her. The gasping for breath, her nails digging into his shoulders, the sweat and heat rolling off their bodies. "Sometimes assertiveness is all about the timing." She pressed her hips against the hardness between his legs. "And this isn't our first time."

She captured his mouth with hers as he buried his

hands in her hair. She wanted to make them both for-get—for just a while—all about the challenges they faced. About Tommy dying. The fire. Her fears. Steve's frustration of fighting a losing battle.

She wanted to lose herself in his strength and warmth. She wanted to remind herself they fit—be-fore and now. She just…*wanted* him. And felt as if she'd waited too many years for him. For this feeling of rightness and completion to move through her.

Hell, to just feel this level of need again.

As his tongue slid over hers, as his fingers finally found her nipples, her body loosened, her pulse beat a rhythm in time to the music and their heartbeats. Cool air flowed through the open windows and top, sending a welcome shiver across her skin.

She helped him slide out of his shirt, pushing it open, then down his arms. She drew her hands down his chest, absorbing the heat and muscle, smiling at his indrawn breath, the way his hands clenched her hips. His fingers moved beneath her dress, along the elas-tic band of her panties, then—as she held her breath—slid beneath them, stroking the heat between her legs.

Dropping her head back, she stroked his shoul-ders, bracing and lifting herself to allow him better access to her femininity. "I'd forgotten," she gasped as he slid his fingers inside her.

His lips found the base of her throat. "I didn't," he said, twisting his fingers.

She moaned, closing her eyes, absorbing every sensation, every pulse. Her desire skyrocketed, tight-ening her stomach, making her clench her fist. "Steve…please."

"My pleasure."

Her breath stopped as he pressed his thumb against the sensitive nub between her thighs.

"Come on, Laine," he whispered against her ear as he stroked her.

She panted to keep up with the tightening pleasure.

His fingers still moved in and out. His mouth moved teasingly along her cheek. "You need this release."

The coil deep within her body flexed, then tightened.

She braced her hands against his chest.

"Come on… *Let go.*"

Her climax exploded within her, sending waves of completion rolling through her body. Her hips jerked. Her head dropped. Her hands trembled.

He held her head against his shoulder, absorbing every pulse. Each sensation.

When she finally came back to herself—and that was a long, hard walk—she planted a kiss on his mouth.

Then she tackled the buttons on his jeans, grasping his hardness between her palms.

His hands flopped by his sides. "Your enthusiasm is appreciated."

She moved her hand down to the seat release, then pushed so they were reclining almost horizontally. She gazed down at him and smiled. "And I haven't even begun."

Grabbing the bottom of her dress, she slipped it over her head, then flicked the front catch of her new black bra and slithered out of her panties.

"Hey, I didn't even—" He stopped when she

tossed the undies aside and pressed her bare chest against his. "So...okay."

She arched her back, longing to feel the full length of him inside her. "Condoms?"

He gasped. "In the console."

She sat up, her hand still wrapped around him. "The console?"

"I bought some yesterday."

"Yeah?" She slid her fingernail around the ridge of his erection. "For me?"

Closing his eyes, he blindly felt around—presumably for the console. "Yes. You wanna help out here?"

She popped open the console, ripped off a foil-packaged condom, then paused as she studied the coil of latex and his erection. She didn't have much experience with this.

He lifted his head. "Problem?"

She glanced from the condom to him and back. "I, uh..."

"Give it to me."

She did, and within a matter of seconds he had the protection in place. "Sorry about that."

He shifted her hips, so they were poised just above him, then eased himself inside her. "I think you're forgiven."

She might have responded—if she were capable of speaking. Instead, she rocked against him. The twist of desire inside her tightened all over again. Ripples of need rolled through her body, clear down to the base of her spine, which she arched to absorb more of him, to cling to the pleasure.

But all too soon, his hips bucked and the tension

inside her broke free again. She braced herself against his shoulders, closing her eyes and absorbing the echoes of their joined orgasms deep within her.

He meant so much more to her than she wanted to admit. His intense focus on her was exhilarating. She admired his longing to be accepted by Aunt Jen, his acceptance of the changes they'd both made in their lives and even his commitment to his jump team.

Was she falling again? Falling for a dangerous, wonderful, risky, dedicated hero?

She really hoped not.

"WELL, WE HAVEN'T LOST our touch there."

Steve kept his eyes closed and tried to calm his breathing. "Like riding a bike."

"Isn't it, though?" She shifted her hips, and he groaned, holding her in place. He wasn't quite ready to break their connection.

Though his body was exhausted, his mind was remarkably sharp. A bold and adventurous Laine was an idea he could embrace. His blood pressure might suffer, but a man had to make sacrifices.

He hadn't expected this overwhelming sense of possession. The thought that he had let her go, that she had undoubtedly shared with other men what they'd just shared, made him break out in a cold sweat. No one else could touch her. He couldn't allow it.

Their time together before had been a source of fun, sex, companionship. He hadn't thought past the upcoming weekend of dates and had resisted her efforts to discuss a future—their future.

When she'd left at the end of the summer, he'd been surprised how strongly her absence affected him. How empty and lost he'd felt. How he'd come to appreciate her need for quiet, her ability to be still. But he'd let his pride convince him he was better off free to pursue adventure and excitement. There had always been another jump, another fire. At least until they dropped into the Cleveland National Forest in the spring, nearly two years after she'd left.

For the first time since then, he was full and whole again, and he had no intention of losing that feeling.

He cupped the back of her head, burying his hand in her hair, bringing her face toward his. "Again."

Her eyes widened. "Ag—"

He captured her mouth, sliding his tongue against hers. His body was already hardening, and she rolled her hips against him in response, sinking him deeper inside. Her body felt so warm, right and soft next to his. She surrounded him, completed him.

As he pumped against her, he closed his eyes, absorbing their link, fighting against the growing need climbing through his body.

He shifted their position, so her breasts dangled above his face. In turn, he sucked her nipples into his mouth.

She gasped. "*Steve…*"

He dragged his mouth along the base of her throat. "Good?"

"Mmm…"

He held her hips still; his erection pulsed inside her. "How good?"

"The best," she panted.

He tongued her ear. "More?"

"Yes." She glared down at him, clearly impatient. "You're fishing for compliments *now?"*

He grinned. "Of course." Actually, he was trying to control his response to her. He wanted them to climax together.

She pulled his hands away from her hips, holding his wrists and pinning them above his head. Then she resumed rocking. "Compliments come later." She slid her mouth across his chest. "If we can still speak later." Her tongue flicked over his nipple.

Closing his eyes, he arched his neck. He wanted to soak up every touch and heartbeat.

Within minutes, though, their heat sizzled through him, his control slipped. Then bottomed out. He held her against him as he peaked and felt her join him as the pulses kicked through his body.

When she collapsed on top of him, he didn't even try to hold back his smile.

AFTER THEY SHARED brownies for dessert, he drove her home. And the kiss he got at the door more than made up for his disappointment the previous night.

When he arrived the next morning at base camp, several guys ragged on him, obviously having heard from Josh and Cole about his date. They tried to pry out details, but he just grinned to himself and shook his head. Last night had been too good, too precious and important to share with anyone but Laine.

As he wandered around looking for Cara, he couldn't help wondering if catching this arson gig would keep him off the backbreaking digs and brush clearing. It almost didn't seem fair.

He found Cara in the mess tent, sharing coffee with the chief and Laine. Obviously, she'd gotten clearance from Cara to come along on the trip to the campsite.

He and Laine had agreed the night before to put on a professional face at the camp, as the work around them was serious and exhausting, and they didn't think it was appropriate for them to be giggling with happiness.

But damned if he wasn't giddy.

He joined the group, sitting across from Laine so he could watch her without being obvious. She was wearing a dark blue shirt and windbreaker, but all he saw was a silky black dress and endless miles of legs that would forever be etched into his memory.

"Our chopper will be here in ten minutes," Cara said.

"Okay." Steve exchanged a glance with Laine, his heart thumping hard and fast when her eyes warmed like whiskey. With remembrance? Anticipation? Either worked for him. "I'm ready when you are," he continued, directing his attention to his sister-in-law, who he suspected wouldn't be fooled for a second by his "professionalism."

"Morning, sir," he said to the chief. "It's all right that I go with Cara today?"

The chief nodded. "In fact, after you direct Cara to the campsite, I'd like you to show Laine the area where you guys put out that hot spot yesterday. Maybe a picture or two will convince the newspapers that we're actually making progress."

"Have they been giving you a hard time, sir?" Steve asked. As much as he didn't like being in the middle of this forest-fire mess again, he recognized the chief's job was a hundred times harder.

"The local news helicopters stay out of the way for the most part, just because they're used to covering fires and know the dangers of stepping over the line. But I've got a couple of guys who think they're going to win a Pulitzer by exploiting a firefighter's death and a town in crisis." His eyes narrowed. "I won't let that happen."

Laine stiffened. "Jeff, I'm not—"

"You should know I didn't mean you." The chief glanced at Steve. "Your personal connection to this fire makes you unique."

"How are the evacuations going, Chief?" Steve asked in an effort to change the subject, in case the chief was talking about him and Laine.

"I'm heading over there this morning to supervise a final check. We expect the fire to reach the Arbor Acres neighborhood by noon."

"How many homes?" Laine asked.

"It's a small community—only twenty. But losing any homes feels like failure."

"At least they have somewhere to go. My aunt said people are flooding into the shelters."

The chief smiled weakly. "I don't know what we'd do without the churches in Fairfax."

"Everybody appreciates your efforts," Laine said. "And you're saving lives—that's the most important thing."

The chief shook his head. "Tell that to your aunt.

She gave me an earful last night about protecting her house."

Laine's neck flushed. "Sorry about that. She's a little…"

"Nutty," Steve said.

"Protective," Laine corrected with a glare in his direction.

A forestry official appeared beside the table. "Captain Kimball, your chopper's here."

They wished the chief a good day, then he and Laine followed Cara to the helicopter. Cara sat in the front next to the pilot, leaving him and Laine to the back. He took the opportunity of helping her fasten her seat belt to stroke the side of her breast. "All set?" he asked softly.

"Keep your hands to yourself, mister." She pursed her lips. "Unless you want a vengeful woman on your hands."

He adjusted the strap, then flicked his thumb across her nipple. "It's a good thing I like to live dangerously."

Her eyes flashed with desire. "I want you, and it's driving me crazy."

He stroked her thigh. "So glad it's contagious."

With incredible reluctance, he dropped into the seat next to her, fastened himself in and put on his headset. Maybe they could do it in a helicopter next. Run through the entire collection of city, state and county modes of transportation.

Oh, yeah. That's a good idea. Real romantic, slick.

They lifted off, and he made an effort to bottle his hot-blooded thoughts. He was already on cushy detail. The least he could do was pay attention.

Evidence of arson, a crime that killed Tommy, might be out there.

For some reason, he didn't really believe that. Maybe because he'd fought countless wildfires, and all of them had started accidentally. Arsons happened, of course. He just didn't have any experience with them.

Though Cara did. She'd been assigned to his hometown of Baxter, Georgia, last fall to lead the investigation into a series of arsons. The town had been consumed by fear and suspicion, while he and his fellow firefighters had been called to raging infernos in the middle of the night. Somehow, amidst the entire mess, she and his brother had gotten together.

He glanced over at Laine, who'd retrieved her camera from her bag and was snapping away through the window. Was the same thing happening to him? Was Laine the love of his life? Could he really feel this happy, this fulfilled, forever?

He'd dated a lot of women over the years. He'd never met anyone he could imagine living with for the rest of his life.

Laine is different, his heart whispered.

Could she be the woman he could share his happiness as well as his pain with? Could he trust her with his secret? Would she understand his fear of forest fires? Would she be glad that he could truly never go back to smoke jumping, or would she think less of him for quitting on his friends?

He shook his head. They were enjoying the moment, the adventure of finding each other again. The rest they'd figure out later.

"We're setting down," the pilot said through his headset.

Steve glanced out the window, spotting the charred area they'd tackled the day before just below him. As the helicopter landed, he reached in the back for the gear—coats, pants, hats and boots. Outside, he helped Laine into hers, then snagged a backpack with a chemical tank while the pilot shut down the engine and radioed their position.

There wasn't much chance of them running into another hot spot today, but he knew being cautious and paranoid about the unexpected had saved more than a few lives over the years.

He smiled at Laine, bundled up in her gear. She looked entirely too small to be able to stand straight, much less walk with all that extra weight. His protective instincts rose at the idea of her tramping around an area that only yesterday was crackling with flames. "Are you sure about this?"

"Yes."

"I could take the pictures for you."

She sighed. "No. You do your job. I'll do mine."

"Maybe you'd be safer—"

Cara shoved lightly at his shoulder. "Where is this campsite?"

Steve pointed toward the trees about fifty feet away. "Through there. Josh and I cut a small path—" He glanced at Laine. "Come on. We'll all go."

"I'm not going," Laine said, setting her camera bag on the ground. "Cara asked me to stay away."

Steve glanced at Cara.

"The campsite is a potential crime scene. I'm the only one taking pictures of it. No press. Even Laine."

"And you're okay with this?" he asked Laine.

"Her pictures are probably going to suck." She grinned at Cara. "Just don't tell my editor how cooperative and understanding I was."

"No problem. Stay off the charred ground until I've had a chance to take some samples. Let's go, Steve." Cara turned and headed toward the trees, her tackle-box crime-scene kit clutched in her hand.

Steve glanced from his sister-in-law to Laine. He had to show Cara the campsite, but he didn't want to leave Laine.

"Will you go?" Laine said as she began snapping pictures of the helicopter.

"Are you sure—" He stopped, not understanding why he was so anxious not to have Laine here. "I know, I know. You're sure. Don't wander off."

"Where would I go?"

Shaking his head at his overprotective instincts, Steve turned and jogged to catch up to Cara. He led her down the trail he and Josh had cut the day before and into the small clearing. He pointed to the right. "I found the gaps made by the tent poles over there."

Cara held out her hand as he started in that direction. "How much walking around did you do?"

"Not much. I walked over by the fire pit, felt the rocks, then noticed the holes a few feet away."

"And Josh?"

"He followed behind me." He looked at her, the way she was staring at the area, and realized he'd probably screwed up. "You're thinking we messed up footprints?"

"With this wind? Probably not. I'm just trying to picture the scene as you found it."

As she dug a small camera out of her kit, Steve watched her work. He admired her focus and attention to detail. The idea that an investigator could uncover a crime with evidence that was literally ashes fascinated him.

"Did you touch the matches?"

"No."

As she knelt by the pit, she drew a pair of surgical gloves from her back pocket and held them out to him. "See what you can find over there."

"Me?"

"You see anybody else?"

He took the gloves, and for the first time, his chest wasn't tight at the thought of doing his job. He didn't feel like a fraud. Or long for escape.

They worked in silence for several minutes, then they strode back to the site of yesterday's hot-spot fire. Laine was kneeling on the ground—well away from the charred ground—still clicking away with her camera.

Cara wandered around the area, and he followed, listening as she pointed out the burn patterns, the spot where she thought the fire had started. Then he helped her take soil samples.

Carried by the winds, sparks from the main fire started almost all hot-spot fires. If that fire was started by an outside source, they should find evidence of an accelerant, such as gasoline or kerosene.

Some time later, they walked back to the chopper. "What do you think?" he asked as Cara stowed the gear.

"Hard to say without the lab tests."

"I didn't smell any accelerant yesterday or today."

"Me neither. The burn patterns look natural. And even if there is a trace of accelerant, finding this guy…"

"Isn't going to be easy."

She sighed, clearly frustrated. "No. Fingerprints on the matches would be nice."

"Maybe it's just some thrill seeker who wanted to observe the fire up close."

"Could be."

"But you don't think so?"

"I don't know what the hell to think." She spun away and walked around to the other side of the helicopter.

He climbed inside, where he spotted Laine settling into her seat.

Smiling, he started to help her fasten her seat belt, but she grabbed his hands. "Oh no you don't. I'm hot, sweaty and cranky. How do you people function with all that suffocating equipment? I thought I was going to melt from the inside out." She plucked her shirt away from her chest, fanning herself with her other hand.

"Should give you a whole new respect for us firefighters."

"No kidding. And there wasn't even a fire out there. I don't know how you guys stand it."

"You get used to it."

She laid her hand along his cheek. "Thank you," she

said, then cut her gaze to the cockpit, where Cara and the pilot were buckling up, and jerked her hand back.

"For what?"

"For doing a job that the rest of us aren't willing to."

Guilt returned and welled up inside him. "It's not that big a deal."

"Yes, it is." Her eyes searched his. "You work hard. And long. It's not just about danger and thrills. It's about dedication and discipline."

He wasn't dedicated, though. He was a fraud. Laine certainly meant to compliment him, but he just felt worse. "I'll pass along your appreciation to the guys."

As he dropped into his seat, he fastened his seat belt, then focused on the scene out the window. How long could he really expect to fool her? How long would it be before he froze attempting to jump out of one of those planes, until he let the uncertainty finally overwhelm him and somebody got hurt—or worse?

He was so focused on his own troubled thoughts that he had to blink several times before the scene below him registered. A man below the chopper was running across a blackened stretch of forest, seemingly headed toward a copse a few hundred yards away. A large duffel bag was thrown over his shoulder, banging against his side as he darted away from the helicopter. He stumbled and fell, then rolled, regained his footing and moved away even faster.

"Set us down!" Cara ordered, obviously noticing the runner.

"There's no room!" Steve barked into the headset before he tossed it aside. He flung off his seat belt, then gathered a rappelling harness and rope. As he slid open the door, he shouted, "Move us over the trees, then hold steady!"

He looked back at Laine. She seemed frozen in her seat, but he couldn't take the time to comfort her now. At the last minute, he caught the walkie-talkie Cara tossed him, then he strapped on the harness, hooking the metal clasp into the overhead buckle and bracing his feet on the chopper's edge.

At the thumbs-up signal from the pilot, he pushed off, releasing the catch on the rappelling gear, his body swinging for several precious seconds in the open air before the rope caught him halfway between the chopper and the ground.

His heart rate zipped into overdrive, his stomach bottomed out, but he pushed aside the distractions and slid down the rope toward the ground. He dropped to the forest floor, then rolled to a crouch. Whoever this guy was, he better hope like hell he was faster than a pissed-off firefighter with a dead best friend.

7

"I LOST HIM."

The dreaded words slid through Laine's headset with a tone of defeat she'd never heard from Steve before. Her heart broke for him.

"And I picked a hell of a time to leave my gun at home," Cara said. "We saw him get onto an ATV, then lost him in the trees. Can you land?" she asked the pilot.

"Not between those trees and the ridge. He'd need to hike a couple of miles."

"Hike?" Laine said, incredulous. "No way." Steve had jumped down there without a thought to his safety or the risk of chasing a possible arsonist, who could be armed with anything. He shouldn't have to hike back to them.

"I agree," Cara said. "Move a little farther away from the trees, and we'll drop the ladder."

"Thanks," Steve said, still sounding out of breath. "I'm not in the mood for a hike."

It was an odd sensation, Laine reflected, hearing his voice in her ears as if he were right next to her, but seeing his tiny figure many feet below them. She could have touched him minutes ago, then he was gone. Memories of rushing to the emergency room where Steve had been taken for smoke-inhalation treatment flashed through her mind.

She'd imagined him doing things like jumping from helicopters, but the reality was much worse. Would she ever close her eyes again and not relive the moment he'd disappeared over the edge? She somehow doubted it.

She was no better equipped to deal with his job now than she had been seven years ago.

"He'll need a hand up," Cara said through the headset before slipping it off. She unhooked her seat belt. "Can you reach a harness?" she shouted over the engine noise as she braced herself between her seat and the captain's.

"Nothing like this ever happened during the Rose Bowl Parade."

"The *what?*"

"Never mind." Laine set aside her camera, which Cara had asked her to use to record the running suspect, then stripped off her own headset and seat belt. Kneeling in her seat, she turned and grabbed a pile of ropes, a ladder and a harness, passing them back to Cara. She tried not to think about the open door and how just a slight tip of the chopper might send both her and Cara plunging to the ground.

When she started to put on a harness, Cara said, "Get back in your seat. I've got it from here."

"You're an arson investigator, not a smoke jumper," Laine said over her shoulder. She didn't want to insult her friend, but neither did she want her risking herself unnecessarily.

"I still do swift-water rescue training every spring. I'll be fine."

Laine buckled her belts. She felt lousy for her fear and completely out of her element. "Great. I'll just do what I always do—watch and record."

She reached for her camera and focused her lens on the edge of Cara's body, to her hand held out to the bright blue sky, her feet braced at the edge of the helicopter.

Laine held her breath, visualizing the moment Steve's head would appear.

And, miraculously, it did.

She snapped several shots—Steve reaching for Cara's hand, her helping him hoist his way over the side, their simultaneous smiles as he stood, steady and whole, inside the chopper next to her. Then his obvious frustration at having lost the man.

As he and Cara found their seats, she put down her camera, unable to resist grasping his hand. He squeezed hers back, and her heart steadied. Finally.

They swept the area several times, all of them on the lookout for the guy and his ATV. Though this wasn't exactly Laine's field, she figured if the man was smart he'd lay low until dark.

Frustration rolled off Steve and Cara in almost visible waves. Laine's stomach had twisted into knots. She could hardly believe what she'd just witnessed. Not just Steve's dramatic rappelling from the chopper, but also the real possibility that the wildfires were being spread by a person, not nature. Someone could be purposely causing the fear, stress, danger and destruction. Letting the fires consume valuable forestland. Destroying property, homes, possessions. Killing—

She gripped the arm of her seat. *Dear God. Tommy.*

By the time they'd gathered in Chief Arnold's tent, she was furious. She paced in front of the desk. "What kind of person does this? It's unconscionable."

"We don't know what he was doing out there, Laine," Cara said, sitting in an ancient-looking aluminum chair, still staring down at the stack of pictures they'd downloaded from Laine's camera to Cara's computer and printed.

Steve crossed his arms over his chest. "He wasn't picking wildflowers."

"I have to agree, Cara," Chief Arnold said, drumming his pen against the desktop.

"What's up with the duffel bag?" Cara asked, turning one picture around and pointing at the close-up of the bag. "What do you think was in it? Did you see it better from your angle, Steve?"

Steve shrugged. "Not really. Just what you see there—dark blue canvas, about two and a half to three feet long."

"Maybe it held the camping supplies," the chief said. "Or clothes."

Cara narrowed her eyes. "Then why would he bother hanging on to it? Steve was chasing him. Why not dump the bag?"

"Maybe it contained ID," Steve said.

That made sense, but Laine could tell the detail bothered Cara.

"Could be," Cara said. "But here's the other thing… Say he is responsible for setting the fire. He does his torch job, hangs around long enough to pitch a tent and watch it burn, then he packs up and leaves. So why did he go back?"

"He left something," the chief said.

"Or," Steve said, "it's what Cara said before—for the thrill."

"Kind of like a killer who visits the grave of his victim," the chief said.

"What does he do?" Steve asked. "Go roll around in the ashes?"

Laine dropped into a chair and leaned her head back. This whole day had drained the energy from her mind and body. "Maybe he films it. Like a movie. You know, so he can look at it over and over."

It took her a few moments to realize the others had gone quiet. She raised her head to find them all staring at her.

"That's not bad," Cara said slowly.

The chief leaned forward. "That could explain why he wouldn't dump the bag."

"And why he went back—he wanted before-and-after pictures," Cara said.

"You mean I helped?" Laine asked.

"Even if you're not right, you've helped," Cara said, staring at her.

Laine rolled her eyes. "Sure I have."

"Can I talk to you outside?" Cara asked.

Laine glanced at Steve, who shrugged, then followed Cara out of the tent.

"Just because you're not the one jumping out of helicopters doesn't mean your contribution isn't important," she said the moment they were alone.

The woman had an arsonist to catch, and she was taking the time to comfort the neurotic photographer. "Believe me, I'm the *last* person who wants to jump out of a helicopter."

"Your pictures may wind up as an exhibit in court one day, you know. I never would have been able to snap clear enough pictures, rattling around in the air like that."

"You looked pretty steady to me."

She shook her head. "I was shaking. Anger, adrenaline, something. Your hands never moved."

Maybe so. And maybe she felt marginally better. But it wasn't her actions that concerned her. It was Steve's. "Your husband is a cop. How do you stand it?"

"I can't ask him to be someone he isn't."

Steve had essentially said the same thing the night before. Was she protecting her heart, or being a stubborn fool?

"I threw up at my first autopsy," Cara said.

Laine laughed. "I'd throw up at *every* autopsy."

"You're not an easy woman to comfort." Smiling, Cara angled her head. "I think I like that about you."

Laine pulled her new friend into a hug. "Thanks for the pep talk."

"Do you love him?"

"Damned if I know."

Cara turned to go back into the tent. "You'll know. Eventually."

"Doesn't mean things will work out."

"No, but it helps."

When they returned to the meeting, Steve and Jeff were studying the photographs. They joined in, and

Laine used her photographer's eye for detail to try to see something the others might not notice.

"Chief?"

They all turned to see a firefighter hovering at the tent opening.

"You have a visitor," he continued.

A second later, a tall, dark-haired man with a close-cropped goatee and striking blue eyes strode into the tent. He headed straight for Cara, pulled her out of her chair and into his arms.

"Show some restraint, for God's sake," she said, trying to escape—though without much force.

He brushed her hair back from her face. "I missed my wife."

"I'm working here."

It was incredibly cute to see solid-as-a-rock Cara flushed and off balance.

"You keepin' her safe?" Wes Kimball asked his brother.

Steve started to answer, but Cara interrupted. "I can take care of myself, thank you."

Wes raised one eyebrow. "Steve?"

"She's bossy, as always, but I was the one who rappelled out of the helicopter."

Steve reintroduced Laine and Wes, introduced the chief, then recounted their day's adventures.

"So where do you go from here?" Wes asked at the end.

"We send the pictures Laine took through the federal database." Cara shrugged. "Wait for the results from the lab on the matches and soil samples."

"Meanwhile, the fire rages on," Wes said.

"Yeah." Jeff rose from his chair. The sprinkling of gray in his hair seemed more pronounced than before, the lines on his face deeper. "Speaking of that…I need to get back there. We've lost eight homes already."

As Jeff shook everyone's hand in turn, Laine hoped those home owners were at least enjoying Aunt Jen's legendary fried chicken. The woman couldn't be convinced to pack and possibly save her own possessions, but had turned her kitchen into a potential Kentucky Fried Chicken franchise.

Maybe nuttiness ran in the family.

When Jeff reached Cara, she said, "You mentioned you're going to run surveillance tonight over the area where the suspect disappeared… I'd like to volunteer."

"I think you've had enough excitement for one day." He walked toward the tent opening. "Rest up for tomorrow."

As soon as he disappeared, Wes pulled Cara back into his arms. "Now that the boss is gone, am I allowed a kiss?"

Cara smiled. "I guess so."

Laine poked Steve in the back. "We'll just go…"

Outside the tent, they were alone for the first time all day. Memories of last night washed over her and her face grew hot.

She looked up at him. "So…nice work today. Though I have to admit, watching you run across that blackened mess and into the trees made my heart nearly explode."

He stiffened. "That's what I do."

"I know." *Boy, do I know.* "I was just worried about you."

"It wasn't that big of a deal." He stared at the ground. "I didn't really think about it. I wish I hadn't lost him."

This modesty was so different from the cocky, thrill-seeking man she'd known that she blinked. She didn't like his tone at all. It was as if he thought he'd failed. "It was amazing. Scary, but amazing."

When he lifted his head, though, he was smiling. "Really?"

"I don't know if I could ever get used to moments like that, but—"

"But?"

"That's who you are."

A weird feeling of contentment moved through her as she said the words. The look in his eyes was different than any other way he'd ever looked at her before. She wanted to say something, to address the moment, but decided the tenderness in his gaze said plenty all on its own.

"It's been a damn long week," Wes said as he and Cara approached. "Let's go out."

Laine and Steve exchanged glances. "No dance clubs," she said.

"I was thinking of your basic bar—a burger, a beer, maybe some pool," Wes said, rolling his shoulders.

"Sounds good to me," Steve said, then slid his hands into the back pockets of his jeans, which stretched his shirt across his broad chest.

Laine's stare shifted from one brother to the other. *Good grief.* She'd forgotten the impact they made. They were sure to send the fan club into a frenzy. "All right. Let's go. But we better grab Cara's gun on the way."

AT SUDS LATER, Steve noted that they made it through the door without a bunch of women surrounding them, but that may have been because of Cara's fierce expression—which Laine had encouraged with tales about the fan club—and her stripping off her jacket to reveal her pistol and shoulder holster.

After they ordered wings, burgers and beer, Wes challenged them to a match of pool—the best three out of five games—with the dinner check on the line.

Steve resisted the urge to glance at Laine as he gravely accepted the bet, knowing without a doubt he wouldn't have to reach for his wallet all night. They flipped a quarter for the break, which he and Laine won.

As he pretended to help her chalk her cue, he whispered, "Can you mess with them a while?"

"Oh, yeah." She angled her head. "I don't suppose they have lobster on the menu?"

Steve glanced around the dark-paneled pool room, the worn orange carpeting and multicolored Christmas lights strewn around the windows. Charmingly tacky was how he'd describe Suds. "In a can maybe."

She wrinkled her nose. "Maybe not."

As he kissed the tip of her nose, he pictured them at a similar bar back home in Georgia. Laughing with his friends, slow dancing on the tiny floor, holding her snugly against him. He'd been striving for a different kind of future for several years now. Had he found it?

"Are you two sure you know which end to chalk?" Wes asked from behind them.

The light of battle slid into Laine's eyes, and she gave him a high five. "Let's dust these guys."

Steve was all for it. Though the amount of money was irrelevant, he was looking forward to being one up on his older brother.

He broke simply because he was afraid, in Laine's zealousness, she might crack the balls a little too hard, and tipping their hand too early would ruin all the fun. He sank a stripe into the far corner pocket, then went for another and missed.

"Too bad, Baby Steven," Wes said as he lined up his shot. "You may never get another chance."

He sank three solids in short order, then smugly stepped back. Steve leaned on his cue as he waited to see what Laine would do in response.

She didn't disappoint, as the cue ball rolled forward about two centimeters when she barely brushed it with the stick.

"Maybe you should help her, Steve," Wes said, his eyes sparkling with obvious pleasure. "I'm not above giving a first-timer some assistance."

Laine looked insulted. "I'm fine."

They went around again, and by the time it was Laine's turn, there were only five balls left on the table.

She leaned over, her face wrinkled in concentration. "I just need to tap it harder."

And boy did she. The cue ball slammed against the three ball, which jumped, hit the side, then sprang off the green, felt-covered table.

Laine was the picture of confused embarrassment. "Okay, maybe not quite that hard."

"This doesn't seem exactly fair," Cara said as she

scooped the ball off the floor and placed it in its original spot.

"Oh, I'll get better," Laine said. "It's just been a while since I played."

"If you're sure," Cara said.

What was this? Honorability in pool?

Not in his family.

Cara sank another ball, Steve missed on purpose, then Wes finished up by clearing out the rest and winning the first game.

As Wes racked up for the second game and continued to taunt him, Steve forgot all about lulling his brother and sinking him later. Wes could be such a pompous ass sometimes. But with anger instead of cool concentration fueling his play—and zero help from Laine—he couldn't beat both Wes and Cara.

"I've had enough," he said to Laine as he pretended to show her how to rack the balls for game three.

"Good. I'm hungry."

"Two to zip is the score, I believe," Wes said, mock pity in his eyes.

"Not for much longer," Steve said, stepping back to let Laine break. "I think Laine's getting the hang of it."

Wes nodded. "I'm sure." Then he burst into laughter.

Cara jabbed her elbow into her husband's stomach. "Quit making fun of Laine."

"Hey, they're gettin' off easy with burgers and beer."

Steve clenched his fist around his cue.

Laine glared daggers at Wes.

Cara shook her head. "You guys are way too into this."

"Maybe we are." Still set up for the break, Laine smiled suddenly at Wes. She never took her gaze off him as she pulled back the stick and slammed it against the cue ball.

The clean, well-scattered break wiped the arrogance right off Wes's face. But only for a moment, since none of the balls dropped into a pocket.

"You're supposed to keep your eye on the ball, Laine," he said, walking over to take his shot.

Cara glared after him. "Cut it out, Wes."

"Oh, he's not bothering me," Laine said sweetly.

When Wes sank only one ball, then he and Cara failed to score, Laine's pleasant expression vanished, and the pool shark Steve knew so well emerged. She proceeded to sink most of the balls on the table, to Wes's growing amazement, then missed on purpose—at least it seemed so—with just three balls left. Having been in Wes's shoes one summer many years ago, Steve caught all the emotions he raced through—confusion, disbelief, determination, amazement.

He figured, at least, that Wes would escape the arousal Steve had felt.

Casting his mind back to that night, he couldn't prevent the quick rush of blood to his head and extremities. He'd taken her to his apartment—and he thought he'd actually said something ridiculous along the lines of "just to talk"—with his senses humming and desire clawing at his insides. She'd been so beautiful, trusting and gentle as he'd hovered over her on his bed. He'd never experienced a moment like that before. In fact, he'd never had an evening like that since—until last night.

Something about the way they fit together trumped everything else he'd discovered in his life. Not even the exhilarating thrill of jumping out of his first plane could compete.

He watched her bend over the table, her jeans pulling tight across her backside and accentuating her curves. She pursed her glossy lips as she popped in the last two solids on the table, smoothly taking game three.

And he realized he was in love.

He had no idea what to do with the emotion coursing through him. Knew even less how to keep from losing it. Laine had shown no sign of wanting their relationship to last beyond their time in California. She might never fully accept his life as a firefighter.

The moment the fire was out, she'd likely leave Fairfax. He didn't want her to go, but had no clue how to get her to stay. Except not put out the fire. And that seemed like a bad idea.

She lulled Wes into thinking he had a prayer in the fourth game, letting them get down to just one ball each plus the eight, before going in for the kill. As she and Wes flipped for the break of the fifth game—which Laine won—the waitress appeared with their dinner. Laine finally quit batting him around and ran the table in a blazing pop of strokes, calling every single shot as she did so.

"Where the hell did you learn to play pool like that, woman?" Wes asked after they'd all climbed into a booth.

"My family owns a bar back home in Texas. I've been playing since I was six."

"You're just lucky she didn't have her cue," Steve said as he wiped chicken-wing sauce off his fingers. "Things might have gotten ugly."

Cara sipped her beer but watched Wes. "Oh, I think it did."

Wes pointed a fry at Laine. "I want lessons."

The guy never could stand being second best.

"Just accept the fact that you were born to be humiliated by women," Steve said. "It must be in your genes."

"Hey, those are your genes, too, little brother."

"No lessons," Laine said. "I need my edge over you people in some area. Besides—" she stared down at her plate "—with the bar closing, I don't know where I'll be practicing anymore. I guess I'll have to find a way to cram the table into my apartment."

Steve thought about the still-unfinished rec room in his basement. A pool table would fit in perfectly with his big-screen TV and lived-in sofa.

"Closing?" Cara asked.

Laine nodded. "The city is widening the road, so we're out, along with several other businesses. The place has been in my family for more than twenty years. I still can't quite accept it."

Seeing the lost expression on her face, Steve's heart dropped. She'd mentioned the bar closing a couple of days ago, but he hadn't questioned her about it. He didn't realize what the place meant to her. The way she'd always talked about it, he assumed she was burdened by her duties as bookkeeper and hold-everything-together girl.

"Couldn't you petition the city?" he asked.

"We tried. We even appealed to the local historical society. Nothing's worked."

"How about busting in there, armed and threatening?" Cara asked.

"Oh, yeah, my sister's done that." Laine paused. "Well, not the armed part, but she comes across with a pretty good threat. It's over."

"I guess you're not okay with that," Cara said.

Shrugging, Laine dipped her fry in ketchup. "I'm getting there."

Later, as they left Suds and parted from his brother and Cara, Steve linked hands with Laine. "Come home with me?"

She glanced up at him in surprise. "Josh—"

"Isn't there." He stopped next to the passenger door of the Jeep and brushed her hair back from her shoulder. "Will you come?"

"Is the same thing going to happen as last time?"

"What last time?"

Grinning, she raised her eyebrows.

"You mean last night?" Using restraint he didn't know he possessed, he opened the door and helped her inside. "Definitely. But I think I can make it home before attacking you."

"You didn't attack me. I attacked you."

"Right." He leaned close, inhaling the sweet, familiar scent of her. "You wanna do it again?"

8

LAINE HELD STEVE'S HAND as she stepped out of the Jeep and onto the sidewalk at the apartment complex.

For some reason, she felt like Cinderella stepping out of a magical carriage. Every glance seemed weighted, every touch heightened. Her skin prickled with anticipation. Her heart pounded with excitement.

He unlocked the door, and they walked inside the apartment, which was as quiet as a church. Her pulse skipped a beat as he closed the door behind them.

When he touched her back, she jumped.

"Are you okay?" he asked against her ear.

"I'm not really sure."

"What can I do?"

She looked around the living room, with its navy recliner and sofa, the silent, big-screen TV. One lamp was illuminated. "It just feels weird. Like we're intruding."

"We're not." He turned her to face him. "Josh was only too happy to find somewhere else to sleep. He was glad to do this for us."

"He probably thinks I'm a bore."

"He doesn't. And if he did, trust me, be complimented."

She drew a deep breath, then forced out the air.

She couldn't explain why she was stalling. She wanted him. He wanted her. Empty apartment. Available bed. Steve had even convinced her to call Aunt Jen and tell her she wouldn't be home until very late.

But every touch they shared, every smile and word and sigh would add up. Eventually, she'd fall completely under his spell again. Then heartbreak wouldn't be far behind.

"Come on," he said, tugging her by the hand toward the hall. "I think you'll be pleased."

When they reached the room at the far end, Steve slid inside first, but he was out quickly, and stood back from the open door and invited her inside.

She walked into a dream. Gauzy, white drapes hung from the ceiling, cascading down to form an intimate tent around the black satin-covered bed. Candles flickered everywhere around the room—tall and short, some in glass holders some bare. Pink and red rose petals were scattered across the floor and bed, and a champagne bucket filled with ice and a bottle sat to the right.

She swallowed the emotion climbing up her throat. "Oh, my."

"I thought we could use an upgrade from the Jeep."

He'd never done anything like this before. In fact, she realized she didn't feel the same sense of unevenness in their relationship she had before. Was that because he was different? Or because she was?

She turned, and he pulled her into his arms. Where everything seemed right. And nothing could possibly go wrong.

"I caught a glimpse of something black and lacy last night, didn't I?"

She leaned back and caught the teasing, hungry expression in his eyes. "You did."

"It was a glimpse."

Sliding out of his arms, she backed away, pulling her shirt over her head as she moved. Steve had never seemed to lack appreciation for her body, and if the clock was really ticking on their time together, she needed to wring every drop from every moment.

He didn't move as she sat on the bed to pull off her jeans.

Clad only in matching black panties and bra, she stroked her hand across the satiny surface of the bed. "Better?"

"I—" He took a step toward her. "Oh, yeah."

As he dropped beside her, she wrapped her hand around the back of his neck, meeting him for a long, deep kiss. "I missed you today."

"You've been with me all but about two hours."

She drew her other hand down the center of his chest. "Not like this."

His eyes blazed, then he pressed his mouth against her cheek, sliding his lips toward her ear, his breath hot against her skin. "You want some champagne?"

"Maybe later."

She threaded her fingers through his hair and inhaled the spicy, musky scent clinging to his skin as she flicked open the buttons on his shirt. Her fingertips slid down his warm chest, across the muscles and sprinkling of hair. He continued placing wet kisses on her jaw and throat.

How many nights had she lain awake and imagined his touch again? Hoped and longed to lay beside him again?

As his hand glided across her shoulder, then down to cup her breast, she arched her back into his touch and decided reality was much better.

"You taste delicious," he said as he leaned into her, laying her back onto the satin comforter.

The scent of roses enveloped her just as the sizzling heat from his body melted her senses. After their frantic lovemaking in the car, she reveled in the slow seduction of his hands and mouth. The flick of his tongue along the edge of her bra. The weight of his legs on top of hers.

She slid his shirt off his shoulders and down his arms, flinging it over her head and onto the floor when he was free. With a twinkle in his eyes, he flipped open the front catch of her bra, helped her out of it, then tossed it aside.

"Just don't let anything hit the candles," she said as she settled back down on the bed. "We'll be calling the fire department."

He propped his head against his hand, then drew one fingertip across her breast. "No department. I'd throw the ice and water from the champagne bucket on the fire."

She sucked in a breath as his finger skimmed her nipple. "That's quick thinking."

"I'm handy that way."

"You won't hear me complaining."

He dipped his head, his tongue encircling her nipple. "I'd like to hear you moaning."

She indulged his request. *Really.* Because the teasing flit of his tongue didn't want to make her moan at all.

Until he did it again. And again...

Clutching his shoulder, she closed her eyes. The intensity of his touch had her body vibrating beneath his hands. Never mind the clothes, her skin caught fire when his breath whispered across her breasts and his hands skimmed down her sides.

The man was an artist. No doubt about it. Probably part of the big, bad, dangerous firefighter code of honor. Distantly, she wondered which chapter this covered.

His tongue swept from her breast to the center of her chest, across her stomach, then dipped into her navel.

"*Steve...*"

He moved, and she opened her eyes as his face appeared above hers. "You called?"

"You were doing fine where you were."

"I intend to do better.'"

Her heart skipped a beat. She wasn't sure she could take better.

She didn't have much choice, though, since he trailed his hand down her body, then slid his fingers beneath the waistband of her panties.

Anticipation and liquid warmth flooded her. The muscles in her thighs clenched.

He teased her with slow, deliberate strokes. She arched her back, trying to press herself more completely into the caress. Her body trembled. She fisted her hands into the satin comforter.

Then he pushed his fingers inside her.

Her hips jumped off the mattress. Her heart rate tripled.

He set a steady rhythm that had her desire cranking up, inch by inch. She arched her back, delighted with his touch, yet needing more. Not wanting the strokes to end, but desperate to find the peak.

"You're flushed," he said against her lips.

"I'm burning up."

He covered her mouth in a kiss, his tongue gliding sensuously with hers. "I want you hotter."

Saying this, he increased the pace, his thumb pulsing with steady pressure at the center of her need.

She panted. She squeezed her eyes shut. Every nerve in her body tightened.

When she finally climaxed, she pulled him against her, holding him tight against her sweat-covered body, wanting him to feel the tiny pulses, the wild thrumming of her heart.

"I can't breathe," she said after her heart had dropped to nearly normal rhythms.

He raised his head, kissed her, then jumped off the bed. "So sorry to hear that," he said as he unbuttoned his jeans and shed them and his underwear all in one motion.

She sat up. "Oh no you don't. I want a repeat."

He dropped onto the bed next to her, pulling her on top of his now-naked body. "Repeating is just what I had in mind."

She drummed her fist lightly against his shoulder. "No." She stopped, considered her response, then corrected, "Well, yes. But I want a repeat of the stripping-off-the-clothes thing."

He laid his hands at the top of her backside, rolling her hips against his, his erection evident. "Maybe later."

Pushing against the bed, she sat up, sliding her legs on either side of him and trapping him snugly between her thighs. "We'll see who's in charge of this."

He raised his eyebrows. "You, it looks like."

She traced her fingertips across his chest, enjoying the smoothness of his skin, the way he hungrily stared up at her. "I'm keeping you prisoner so you can't go back to work."

"I'm fine at work, Laine."

"I worry. I told myself I wasn't going to, but I do anyway."

He slid his palms across her thighs, holding them in place, pressing the heated center of her body against his hardness. "I'm careful."

Some part of her recognized she shouldn't have brought this up. She was taking a chance on an affair, not a future.

What if I could accept his job, though? A job he loves, that he has to do? What if, despite the danger, the uncertainty, I could take a chance on love again? And what if...what if I'm just using his job as an excuse, a reason not to risk my heart?

She didn't want to think about those questions. She wanted to consider the answers even less.

His gaze fixed on hers, he reached up and cupped the back of her neck. "I need you, Laine."

She wouldn't have denied that request for anything.

She laid her body across him, rubbing her breasts across his chest, rolling her hips against his.

He groaned and grabbed her sides, holding her tight against his erection. "Condoms."

"Where?" she breathed against his neck.

"My jeans."

In the process of flicking her tongue across his earlobe, she stopped. "They're on the floor."

A long pause ensued. Finally, he groaned. "I'll—"

"I'll get them." She pushed herself off his body, both of them moaning at the loss of heat and connection. After fumbling through the pockets of his jeans, she managed to snag a trio of foil pouches.

Might as well be prepared.

As she climbed back on top of him and flipped her hair back, she tore off one packet, pulled out the condom, then rolled it on swiftly.

His eyes fluttered closed. Tension lined his face. "That was…unexpected."

"I was paying attention last time."

"So glad to hear it."

She angled her head, though she recognized he couldn't see her. "That feels good—me taking the initiative?"

He raised his hand, his thumb and index finger just an inch apart. "A bit."

"Really?" She rolled her shoulders back, arching her body against his, feeling the slick warmth of her body glide over his hardness. She'd never really considered that before—well, she knew men liked women touching them—she'd just always felt some measure of embarrassment with the issue of protection. After all, that led to discussions of past sexual

history, fear of pregnancy and so on. All mood kill-
ers in her opinion.

"Laine?"

"Uh huh?"

"Could we get on with this now? I'm suffering
here."

Glancing down at him, she recognized the
strained expression on his face. "Oh. Well—"

With a shift of their hips, he pushed inside her.

She arched her back and braced her hands against
his chest as he filled her with a completeness she
could never describe to anyone. Just a sense that the
passion was right, a sweet idea that they were meant
for each other. "Oh…"

"Well," he finished.

Speaking after that moment wasn't possible.

He held her hips. She arched and lifted against
him. His skin glowed with sweat as they moved together, as they strained toward mutual peaks. When
she finally came, Steve was with her, pumping his
body against hers, holding her to his heart.

STEVE HELD LAINE'S sleeping body closely by his side.
He should be exhausted, and though he was physically
drained, his mind was alert. Worrying. Wondering.

She'd shared her body and her touch. She'd
laughed and moaned. She'd seemingly given herself
to him completely. But her eyes still held reservations and distance.

Not that he could blame her. He hadn't given her
any reason to trust him again. When they'd dated before, he'd played at being her lover. He'd said the

right things and had fun. He'd given her his body, but not his heart.

He also had to admit, in the silence and the dark where no one could see him, that he wasn't comfortable lying to her every day, pretending total commitment to fighting this fire. He wanted to help Cara with her investigation, to find the man who might be responsible for Tommy's death, but he wanted nothing to do with rappelling, jumping or hacking his way through that forest.

In the years since he'd retired from smoke jumping, he'd spent many hours searching his heart for why he couldn't stomach the business anymore. Did he fear death? He certainly didn't want to die.

But in his business, in his family, fear wasn't acceptable.

And in the ensuing years after he'd left California, he'd crashed through the doors of burning buildings many times without the slightest hesitation.

Part of his lack of interest in jumping had been frustration. Once you survived training, there wasn't much thought in fighting wildfires. A plan of attack was determined almost instantaneously after a call came in. The execution was second nature, mindless and often monotonous. Trekking through the woods for days, fueling yourself with the thought that you might be the only line of defense for an endangered community.

He liked strategy. He liked the sense of community that came from working in a local fire department. Interacting with the people in his hometown. Not just his fellow firefighters, but the teachers and students at the schools where he visited several times a year to talk about fire safety.

He liked the details of arson investigation. The one thing that had made the last couple of days bearable was working with Cara. Of wondering about motivations and strategizing about how to get the answers they wanted.

Maybe he was simply a different man than he'd been seven years ago. Maybe no better or worse.

But he still couldn't escape the thought that he'd let Tommy down by not being there for him. He should have been able to save him. He'd deserted his team and friends long ago, and he didn't belong with them now.

There was no running from that fact—no matter how hard and fast he wanted to.

Laine stirred beside him, her hand sliding across his chest. "What time is it?" she asked sleepily.

He glanced at the digital clock on the bedside table. "Three."

She stiffened, then sat up. "I should go."

His heart contracted at the sight of her naked silhouette. He reached up and pushed her tangled hair away from her face. "You don't have to." He didn't want her to.

She scooted across the bed away from him. "I need to go," she said as she stepped into her jeans.

Distance again. He set his jaw and said nothing, reaching for his jeans.

Tell her how you feel. How do you expect her to stay with you when you won't share even that much? She needs to know how important she is to you.

Ignoring his conscience, which obviously hadn't realized his feelings were the least of his problems, he shrugged into his wrinkled shirt, then dug his keys from his pocket.

Laine approached him with her sandals dangling from two fingers. She raised on tiptoe and kissed him. "Where did you go?"

Knowing she expected—and needed—the easygoing playboy, he forced a smile and grabbed her around the waist. "I'd like to go back in that bed."

"And risk Aunt Jen coming after you with a crowbar?"

He peered down at the cleavage revealed by her shirt. "Might be worth it."

She tugged him out of the room. "Come on. We've both got a long day tomorrow."

"You mean today."

She groaned. "Any chance for coffee and doughnuts delivered at seven?"

"Nope. I've got to be on scene at seven."

On the ride back to Aunt Jen's, they talked about their worries for the town, the loss of the homes at Arbor Acres, the possibility of rain in the forecast, and speculated about the mysterious man he'd chased.

She didn't say anything about her feelings changing, that she wanted anything more than they had. He kept quiet as well. While he doubted his abilities as a smoke jumper, he couldn't give up firefighting. He couldn't imagine ever saying no to someone who needed those particular skills.

But if he said that to her he'd mess everything up—again.

At the door, she kissed him, then whispered, "Be careful," before she slipped inside the house.

On his way to base camp later that morning, he wondered if that was his problem. Was he being *too* careful? Could he really let Laine leave Fairfax without telling her how he felt?

When he reported for work, he learned Cara was waiting for him in Chief Arnold's tent.

"Where's Wes?" he asked as he strode inside.

"Are you kidding? He's asleep."

"He's delicate and needs his rest," he said, bringing a grin to her lips. "Any word on the identity of our guy?"

She raised her eyebrows. "He's *our* guy now, huh?"

He couldn't do much for Tommy, but he could do this. "I want to help."

"Convenient. I need your help."

"Now?"

"Yes, now. You have other plans?"

He glanced out the door. Josh and the others were probably getting into their gear by now. "I'm supposed to be on the front line today."

"Not anymore. The chief has assigned you to me."

Before he could do more than suppress a pop of excitement, she handed him a stack of photos. He recognized them as the ones Laine had taken yesterday. The images had been sharpened, the profile of the man's face blown up to an eight-by-ten and printed on high-quality photo paper.

"I picked these up from the print shop this morning," she said. "As you can see, they're much better quality than the ones I made yesterday with my portable printer. See anything that strikes you as familiar?"

He studied all three pictures. Other than yesterday, he'd never seen the guy, but he did notice his nose was distinctive—a bit too large for his face, with a hump on the bridge, like an incorrectly healed break. "Nothing familiar."

"Unfortunately, the FBI thought the same thing."

"No criminal record?"

"None."

"The nose is memorable, though. Maybe somebody in town saw him."

"My thoughts exactly." She rose from her chair. "What do you think about starting with the sporting goods stores?"

In a town the size of Fairfax there were only two stores that sold camping equipment, so it didn't take long to get a hit.

"Oh, yeah, I remember him," the clerk said, staring at the photos from behind silver-rimmed glasses. "He came in early last week. Kind of odd looking. Didn't say much. Usually when people buy equipment, they can't stop talking about their trip, always asking for the best spots for fishing and hunting. I usually send 'em to Ned Walter's place up on—"

"Mr. Jennings, did he by chance pay with a credit card?" Cara asked, her patience obviously short.

"Nope. Cash. That was another odd thing. He bought a lot of stuff with a big wad of cash."

"Did he say anything that might give you a clue to who he was or what he did?" Steve asked.

"Nope." He handed back the pictures. "Like I said, he didn't talk much."

"What about other details?" he asked. "Like his hands, were they clean? Were his nails ragged? What kind of car did he drive?"

"I don't remember anything about his hands. The car, I noticed. Big black SUV. Chevy, I think."

Steve started to press for more, but he added, "And no, I didn't get a tag number. You two sure are anxious. What's this fella done?"

"Thank you for your time," Cara said, laying her card on the counter and a smaller copy of the close-up photo. "My cell-phone number is on the back. If you think of anything else, please call me."

As they left the store, Steve considered what they'd learned. The guy was bold enough to buy camping equipment locally, but wise enough to pay with cash. The purchase also seemed to indicate a lack of planning. After all, if he'd come in to town intending to camp out at a fire scene, why didn't he bring his own equipment? And he sensed the guy was an outsider; otherwise, the clerk probably would have recognized him.

"The question about the hands was good," Cara said as they climbed into her rental car. She glanced casually over at him. "You ever thought about joining the investigation side of this business?"

"Not until last fall. I was really into that case you and Wes handled."

"Let's hope we don't run into a mess like that again anytime soon—at least not at home."

"It's back to normal now. Boring."

"Unfortunately, there's plenty of work," Cara said. "I could put in a word for you with the state investigative branch."

"Okay," he found himself saying. And the more he thought about the idea, the better he liked it. Would Laine like it, as well? Could this be the compromise they could both embrace?

Though he wouldn't be a day-to-day firefighter, he'd have to be honest about his willingness to lend a hand when he was needed. If they could settle that…would she feel more comfortable with his career?

What if he followed her back to Texas? Or she moved to Georgia?

He took the fantasy further. Him, a husband to Laine, a father to their children. Him, an arson investigator, combining the excitement he once craved with the mature stability he now required.

How can you plan a future when you haven't faced the past?

He ignored his conscience. He wouldn't have to come back to Fairfax or smoke jumping. Laine, Josh, Cole nor anybody else ever had to know about his fears.

"You'll have to hit the books for a while," Cara said as she pulled into a parking place in front of a local diner. "Arson investigating is a weird balance between science, firefighting and law."

"I can do that."

"There's something else…" She tapped her fingers on the steering wheel, as if trying to decide whether to proceed. "You know I don't pry into other people's love lives."

"Yeah."

"Okay. Here's the thing…have you told Laine you're in love with her?"

He whipped his head toward her. "Have I *what*?"

"I've been looked at the way you look at Laine by one of you Kimball brothers, you know, so I recognize the signs. Though, admittedly, it took me a while to realize it."

"Did it?"

"Yeah. So, anyway, you're gonna tell her, right?"

He said nothing for a moment, angling his head as he considered her advice—which, of course, he'd already decided to pursue on his own. And to hear Cara toss back his feelings so succinctly made him even more determined to figure out where he stood with Laine.

"I'll tell her eventually."

"Dammit, Steve, now's not the time to hold back. You have to go after love like you jump out of planes—quick and all the way."

Amused, he leaned back against the car door, facing her. "That's kind of poetic."

She kicked the door open. "Fine. Make fun of me. But when you're old and gray and despondent, don't come running to me. I'll just shoot you and put you out of your misery."

He popped out of the car and eyed her over the roof. "Aw, that's very sweet."

She pointed at him, her eyes swimming with anger. "You want my recommendation into the arson division?"

"You want to be a bridesmaid?"

She threw up her hands in disgust and stomped toward the diner's front door, which he opened. "I'm not talking to you."

"How about a godmother?"

"Let's see you get the girl first, big boy."

They weaved through the crowded, noisy diner and settled at the counter. Cara especially got a few odd glances—no doubt due to the pistol strapped to her side.

"What are we doing in here, by the way?" he asked Cara.

"Having lunch." Her gaze swept the room. "And talking to the locals."

After the indulgent night of burgers and beer, they ordered the blue plate special of stewed chicken and steamed vegetables. As Steve sipped his soda, he watched the people around him. Some smiled as they dug in to their meals, but most were visibly tense, with the fire being the chief topic.

Without the much-needed rain, the fire would surge past the outlying areas and consume the very heart of the town. He couldn't imagine walking through the rubble of this busy diner, ash strewn across the floor where waitresses once rushed with comfort food.

When his cell phone rang, he flipped it open and noticed a local number on the ID screen. Not Laine. Or Aunt Jen. "Hello?"

"Steve, this is Chief Arnold."

"Yes, sir?"

"You need to get to Fairfax Memorial right away. Josh has been hurt."

9

"I'M IN TROUBLE," Laine said to Denise as they helped the United Methodist Women's Group—of which Aunt Jen was the president—clean up the lunch they'd just served to the fire refugees. "I'm in love."

Elbow-deep in soap suds and pans, Denise frowned. "Why is that a bad thing?"

"You didn't see him rappel out of a helicopter yesterday."

"I thought he'd given that up."

"Apparently not." And beneath the surface of his dangerous job, of the obvious love he had for firefighting, she knew something else was bothering her. Something she didn't want to acknowledge, because then she'd have to label herself a hypocrite. Her conversation with Steve the night of the picnic was coming back to haunt her.

"Is it really the rappelling that bothers you?" Denise asked.

Leave it to a friend to tell you what you didn't want to hear. "Shouldn't it?"

"You don't have to like it. But if you love Steve, you have to accept it."

Laine was fairly certain Denise and Cara must

have gotten together to give the same advice, but she wasn't sure how to prove it. "But—"

"And if you expect him to give up his job, you have to be willing to give up yours."

"I what?"

Denise tossed her rag in the sink and planted her hands on her hips. "Where were you during this rappelling thing?"

"In the helicopter taking pictures."

"Sounds pretty dangerous to me."

"It's not. It's entirely different. For one, my editor made me."

"I thought you said this pictorial on the wildfires was your idea. So you could keep money coming in for you and your sister. So you could work and still look after Aunt Jen."

Laine turned away and dropped silverware into the dishwasher. "Well, it was, but I was planning pictures of people evacuating, the shelters—a human-interest thing—and my editor—"

"So you're doing something that's sort of dangerous, but necessary to do your job. And you're doing it to ensure someone else's safety." Denise pursed her lips. "Why does that sound familiar?"

That's exactly what Steve does.

Denise didn't have to say the words for Laine to hear them. And he didn't do his job recklessly or thoughtlessly, but heroically.

"So maybe it's not the job!" Laine slammed the dishwasher shut and whirled to face Denise. "Maybe the job is just an excuse for protecting myself. I loved him before, and he didn't love me. At least not enough. As a matter of fact, he decided he'd rather jump out of planes into big, raving waves of fire than be with me.

"I got involved with him again because I told myself it didn't matter what he did, that I wouldn't fall for him. I didn't want my heart broken again! Is that so wrong?"

Denise stepped toward her, enveloping her in a hug. "No, it's not." She ran her hands soothingly across her back. "You're naturally cautious and responsible, Laine. Growing up with your sister, I guess you had to be."

Actually, Laine had spoken with her sister earlier in the day to apologize for being so snappish lately, and she'd learned Cat was taking greater responsibility of the bar—and her life.

"I know you're worried about Steve," Denise went on, "but you'd worry about him no matter what he did. That's what you get with love."

"That's why I don't want it," Laine said, disgusted with herself for whining.

"I'm betting you'll change your mind. I think you guys can make it work this time."

Though her doubts and fears still pressed on her, Laine at least realized there was no turning back now. She loved Steve. Had from the moment she'd met him. Probably always would.

"Thanks," she said. "You're a good friend."

"I'm a friend who has definite ideas about her bridesmaid dress." Leaning back, Denise grinned. "I'm thinking a slinky fabric, an icy color. Maybe pale blue or green. How do you feel about miniskirts?"

"I feel like you're getting way too ahead of yourself."

"How's the cleanup going?" Aunt Jen asked as she marched into the kitchen.

Laine peered around Denise. If nothing else, this trip back to California had connected her with Aunt Jen again. Over the years, she'd worried about her mother's sister. She'd never married and at times seemed to have only her dolls and antiques for companionship.

"We're done," she said to her aunt.

"Laine's in love," Denise said at the same time.

Laine frantically shook her head at her friend, but it was too late, the light of battle had sparked in her aunt's eyes.

"I suppose this has something to do with that boy who ruined my roses."

"That was seven years ago, Aunt Jen. Don't you think it's time to let it go?"

"No. He didn't treat you right. He made you cry."

Laine swallowed. Aunt Jen had heard her cry? She wasn't sure if she was humiliated or touched. Both, maybe. "I'm fine now. Don't go reaching for the crowbar."

She waggled her finger. "You just make sure he knows I'm watching him."

"Isn't the evacuation awful? My parents are beside themselves trying to pack everything up," Denise said, laying her hand on Jen's arm.

Poor Denise probably thought she was steering them away from a touchy subject, but Laine knew the evacuation was an even bigger issue for her aunt.

She lifted her chin. "I'm not leavin' yet."

Denise cast an uncomfortable glance at Laine. "But the order went out for tomorrow morning."

"That's tomorrow morning. We're gettin' rain. I can feel it in my bones. We won't need to evacuate."

Not that she was against the bone method of weather forecasting, but Laine had packed her bags anyway. The challenge would be to convince her aunt to do the same thing. "If it's not raining by six, I'll help you pack."

Aunt Jen shook her head. "Nope. We might jinx the rain."

"*Jinx* the rain?"

"And no more talk about packing." She turned toward the door. "As a matter of fact, I think I'll call the prayer group together. Your lack of faith could mess up my plan."

Laine shook her head as she watched her go. "I guess I'd better get home before she does."

"Why?" Denise asked.

"To hide the suitcases I packed this morning under the bed."

"Definitely a good idea. Is it really supposed to rain?"

"Twenty percent chance."

Denise winced, then she started toward the door.

"Where are *you* going?"

"The prayer group. They need all the help they can get."

Laughing, Laine finished straightening up the kitchen. She had no idea where she was going to find the courage to tell Steve about her feelings, but if Aunt Jen was determined to face down a wildfire and the wrath of heaven, she supposed she'd have to try.

As she was heading out, her cell phone rang. "Hello?"

"Laine, it's Cara. I'm at Fairfax Memorial."

Her heart kicked against her chest. "Steve?"

"No, it's Josh."

STEVE LEANED BACK against the tiled wall in the emergency room as Cara paced beside him.

"Idiot," she muttered.

"Just too gung-ho," Chief Arnold said. "That's Josh."

Josh had been working on reinforcing the firewall when a large branch had fallen from a burning tree. Instinctively, Josh had shoved a fellow smoke jumper out of its path and taken the blow himself.

His arm was broken and doctors suspected a concussion. But since he was still unconscious and undergoing tests, they weren't saying much.

I should have been there.

Steve couldn't get that one refrain of regret out of his mind. Instead of helping his buddies, he was happily interviewing sporting goods store clerks. Yesterday, instead of fighting the fire, he was tramping through an abandoned campsite.

He glanced at the rest of the team, sitting in a row of chairs just a few feet away beside Josh's parents. He had to stay away from them. He couldn't face them. Or Josh.

"One of the teams reported rain," the chief said into the quiet. "Not much to make a difference. But it gives people hope."

"Steve and I found out more information about our mysterious runner," Cara said, then updated the chief on their morning.

"He doesn't seem to be making much effort to hide himself," the chief said. "That doesn't seem—"

He stopped as a large group of women stormed through the emergency-room doors. Laine and Aunt Jen were leading the pack.

"How is he?" Laine asked, grabbing Steve into a hug before he could do more than stare at all of them in surprise.

"Critical still. How did you find out?"

"Cara called me."

He glared in his sister-in-law's direction, though she just shrugged, apparently unrepentant. "I wouldn't have wanted to worry you. And what are they doing here?" he added in a lower tone.

She leaned back, cupping his face between her palms. "The prayer group."

"I had to pull them off rain duty," Aunt Jen added.

He really didn't have the strength or patience for her today. "Rain duty?"

"They're praying for rain," Laine said, finally letting go of his face but keeping a tight hold on his hand.

Though he was humiliated that he longed for her strength, he let it seep into his body. He needed her so much. And didn't come close to deserving her. She'd toasted him as a hero once, but he certainly wasn't. A hero didn't run from his fears. He faced them.

He wanted to be the kind of man she deserved, the kind of man she needed him to be.

By now, the other women had gathered close to

the rest of the team, and they were all holding hands and bowing their heads.

Aunt Jen looked him up and down. "You look like you escaped fine."

"I've been with Cara all morning, working on the investigation."

"I like that idea much better personally," Laine said, watching him closely, as if she knew the conflict inside him. "I kept picturing you in the ambulance beside Josh."

"I doubt I was in much danger in the sporting goods store."

The harsh tone of his voice had Chief Arnold and Aunt Jen staring at him. Cara stopped pacing.

Laine squeezed his hand. "I think I'll go get some coffee for everyone. Want to help?"

"I'd rather—"

"I really need your help." She tugged him away from the group and down the hall, then outside through a back door.

Judging by the crushed cigarette butts littering the pavement, he assumed this was the area where hospital workers sneaked outside for a smoke.

Laine faced him, crossing her arms over her chest. "What's wrong?"

The simmering fury in his chest exploded. "One of my closest friends nearly got killed! Other than that, everything's just great."

"I know what's wrong with Josh. What's wrong with you?"

"You're trying to piss me off."

"No, you're doing just fine with that on your own."

"Go away, Laine. You don't want to be around me right now."

"You're wrong," she said softly. "There's no place in the world I want to be more than right here."

"Then I'll leave." He flung the door open and stormed inside.

You're running again.

He didn't care. He just knew he couldn't face Laine. Or anybody else.

When he reached the end of the hall, he passed the admissions desk, where a man with crutches tucked beneath his arms was talking to a nurse.

He scooted around the guy, wondering if the chief would let him work the fire—

Slamming to a halt, he spun around. The guy with the crutches had a cast on his foot and wore a baseball cap. A duffel bag sat at his feet. He glanced Steve's way, then looked away quickly.

Too quickly.

In an instant, he'd grabbed the guy's shoulder. He stared down into his face and knew right away he was facing the runner from the forest. The one who'd stumbled and fallen. And still managed to escape.

The guy tried to wrench his way free, though Steve was much larger and stronger. "Hey, man! Take your hands off me!"

Heart pounding with satisfaction and anger, Steve shook his head. "No chance."

The nurse picked up the phone. "I'm calling security."

"Be my guest," Steve said, then shouted over his shoulder. "Cara!"

A second later she rounded the corner, Chief Arnold just behind her. "What the hell…"

"Our good friend from the forest seems to have injured himself," Steve said. He nudged the bag at his feet. "What's in the bag?"

"My…equipment," the man said, his gaze darting from Cara to the chief to Steve.

Steve grabbed the guy by the front of his shirt. "What equipment?"

"Good grief."

Steve turned as he heard Laine's voice. Her face suffused with concern, she jogged toward them. "What happened? What's going on?"

"I have credentials," the man said, leaning back so far he was nearly lying on the admissions desk. "And the First Amendment."

"The First—" Chief Arnold began, glancing at Steve.

Steve let go of the guy long enough to kneel and unzip the bag. Inside was a camera and tripod.

"He's not an arsonist," Laine said, staring down at the camera. "He wants a Pulitzer."

"Arsonist?" The guy's eyes nearly bugged out of his head. "You people are crazy."

Cara flipped open her badge. "You were seen yesterday at a fire scene. A fire that took the life of a firefighter the week before. You could be charged with trespassing. At the worst, murder. I'd advise you to start talking."

NEWTON GRANGER, staff photographer for the *Los Angeles Times*, talked fast.

Laine sat in fascinated silence during the questioning as he waived his right to an attorney, agreed to be taped and blabbed out everything from his shoe size to what he'd had for breakfast three weeks ago last Sunday.

Newton, it seemed, was tired of being low man on the totem pole at the newspaper and figured his ticket out of obscurity was a set of pictures that would awe the world. But instead of stalking celebrities like most photographers in L.A., he was stalking a fire. He figured he could camp out in the forest and get the pictures of his life.

He claimed he hadn't set any fires, and for the most part Laine thought everyone believed him, but it was also possible that a spark from his campfire had ignited one of the hot spots—especially given the proximity of the campsite they'd inspected yesterday.

No matter how you looked at it, the guy was in loads of trouble.

"And if you'd been trapped by the fire? What would you have done then, Mr. Granger?" the chief asked, his expression betraying his disgust.

"I had flares and a cell phone," Granger said.

"Which you could use to call me and my teams of firefighters to save your sorry butt." The chief rose, shaking his head. "Call the FBI, Cara. Have them pick him up. They should be able to hold him until the tests come back and we can figure out if Granger's campfire caused the hot spot."

Along with Steve and Chief Arnold, Laine left the small examining room the hospital had let them use to conduct the interview. It seemed as though

Tommy's death really had been an accident, though that seemed to bring no one any comfort.

"I'll go see if there's any word on Josh," the chief said as he strode off.

She and Steve were left alone with an awkward silence. His anger had surprised her. She'd never thought of him as having much of a temper. He was almost always smiling, teasing and easygoing.

"I'm sorry," he said finally, pulling her into his arms. "I had no right to talk to you the way I did."

"It's okay. You were upset about Josh."

"Yes. No. That wasn't it, I mean."

"Then what was it?"

He held her head against his chest for several long minutes. "I should have been there to help," he said finally.

"You were helping. You were with Cara."

"Holding the door for her. Any idiot could have done that."

She leaned back and looked up at him. She didn't like the expression on his face—harsh, almost bitter. "She wouldn't have asked you if she didn't need you specifically."

"I should have been with the team."

"Doing what? From what I've seen, you guys are more like glorified ditch diggers than anything else these days. It looks backbreaking to me. Why—" She stopped. "You think you could have saved him."

"Probably not. Maybe." He sighed. "They still deserved my back and my loyalty."

Several things she'd assumed suddenly didn't seem quite so certain. She'd thought Steve was having a great time being back with his team, jumping from planes and fighting the very essence of nature. But whenever he'd had the opportunity, he'd chosen to work on the investigation. Yesterday was his off day, so she figured he just wanted to be with her, but now she realized there was more to his decision.

She also realized she'd never asked him a very important question. "Why did you give up smoke jumping?"

He stiffened. "You go right for the bottom line, don't you?"

"Any reason why I shouldn't?"

"No, there's just not an easy answer."

"I'm not going anywhere."

He slid his hand against hers. "Let's take a walk outside."

On the way out front, they passed Chief Arnold, who told them Josh was stabilized and being moved to a room. They would be allowed to see him later in the afternoon.

The good news did nothing to dispel Steve's melancholic mood, though. They walked out the doors and past the main driveway to a grassy area on the hospital grounds.

"In the spring, almost two years after you left, we were called to the scene of a fire in Cleveland National Forest." He stopped walking and stared off in the distance, as if he could still see the scene before his eyes. "David Holt and I were hacking our way along a ridge, when the ground collapsed beneath us. I rolled down the hill and broke my leg in two places. He was cut pretty badly by the hacksaw he was using."

Laine closed her eyes briefly, but said nothing, hurting for him and sensing the need for him to get through the story without interruption.

"He helped me hobble to a small cutout in the mountain, a tiny cave neither of us could stand in. I bandaged his arm, and we, of course, called for help.

"Unfortunately, by the time the other guys got to us, the fire had intensified and shifted in our direction. We were trapped.

"It seemed to take forever for reinforcements to arrive and a helicopter to drop water on the fire, but I found out later it was less than an hour. The whole time the flames crept closer, I kept seeing visions of my family back in Georgia, the lake where I'd always planned to build a house." He stroked her face. "I even wondered what would have happened if I'd taken you up on your offer to leave that summer."

"You mean my ultimatum to leave."

"At that moment, retirement was looking like a pretty wise option." He held her hand in his and started walking again. "For a while after we were rescued and I had healed, I forced myself to keep going, but I realized I was making a mockery of everything my team stood for, so I quit."

"And you're ashamed of that?"

"Yes."

Now that the story was done, she wrapped her arms around his waist, reminding herself he was whole and alive, comforted herself with the steady beat of his heart. "But you came back and did it again anyway. And why…" She lifted her head and met his stark blue gaze. "In Tommy's memory. To help your friends."

"And I hate every minute of it."

Her eyes watered. "That's the bravest, most heroic thing I've ever heard."

"No, it's not. I'm betraying everything they stand for."

"You *are* everything they stand for. You're facing down your fears. You jumped out of a helicopter to chase a suspect. What more do you expect yourself to do?"

"I didn't do anything. I lost him."

She waved her hand. "And caught him today."

"Luck. I practically tripped over the guy."

Laine ground her teeth. The man was so aggravating. How could she possibly love someone so stubborn?

"I used to live for moments like rappelling from that chopper. The team still does live for moments like that. Josh and the others wouldn't be able to look me in the eye if they knew."

"Who's telling them? Not me."

"*I* know!"

She glared at him. "So it's your guilt and not their judgment that you're really worried about. What did you tell Josh and the others, by the way?"

"That the doctor advised me to give up jumping."

"And did he?"

"Yes."

She threw up her hands. She also rashly decided she needed something to shock the man out of this ridiculous self-deprecating attitude. "Well, how's this for truth—I'm proud of you. For knowing you needed to retire, for being brave enough to come back when you were needed."

"I'm not being brave, I—"

"And I love you."

10

"I'm still a firefighter, you know," Steve managed to say.

"I know."

Just a few hours ago, he'd figured out a compromise he obviously didn't need. He'd made plans. He'd envisioned a future. All he needed was her love.

"Do whatever you like," she continued, "smoke jumping, axing your way through doors, saving cats from trees. I'll still love you."

Tell her. Tell her, you idiot. You love her, don't you? Grab her and run like crazy back home.

But he just couldn't do it. He'd run for too long.

"So what do we do now?"

"I have no idea." He was frozen into a state of shock. She knew his secret, and she still loved him.

"You know, I imagined this moment much more romantically."

He yanked her into his arms and kissed her with all the confusion and love trapped inside him. When his need for her washed over him, he couldn't remember anything else, he couldn't think or concentrate on anything but her. It was, in a way, an escape. And he couldn't use her like that.

"That was a definite improvement," she said when they came up for air.

"Yeah." But he released her and stepped back. He was numb and cold—not in his heart, where she dominated his feelings—but throughout the rest of his body. He felt the way he did the moment they pulled him out of that cave and lifted him into a chopper. As if he knew nothing would ever be the same.

"I know it's been a w-wild day," she said, her voice hitching a bit. "Really a wild few days. But when I leave here, I want you to go with me."

She wanted a future with him.

But he couldn't escape the feeling that he was cheating her. That he couldn't be whole and devoted to her until he faced his fears, until he faced Josh and the rest of the team honestly.

To be the kind of man she thought he was. The kind of man he wanted to be for her.

"I—"

I'm proud of you.

She thought he was brave. He wasn't.

"I'm not the man you think I am."

She stroked his face. "I think you're strong and loving and brave."

"I'm not. I'd like to try to be, but—"

Could he really tell Josh about his fears? And even if he could and his reaction was similar to Laine's, could Steve forgive himself? Accept himself?

He stepped back. "I need to go. I need to do something." Uncertainty about himself, what he'd done and had to face crashed over him. "They're digging a new trench this afternoon to try to protect

Aunt Jen and her neighbors. With Josh hurt, they need help. I want to be there."

Though hurt and confusion swam into her eyes, she nodded. "You'll come by the house later?"

"Sure." He backed away from her. "I need to go."

You're running...

He raced back to the camp and loaded up his gear, then sped to the front line. He gave Aunt Jen's house, just on the other side of the ridge where they were setting up the fire wall, no more than a passing glance, but inside he burned with conviction. That house would still be standing tomorrow, and the next day, and the next day...

Part of him knew he couldn't single-handedly stop the fire, but he would be part of the effort to do so, no matter how much the past tried to overwhelm him, no matter what they asked him to do.

No one questioned his appearance, just asked for the status on Josh. They'd all been there—lost a colleague, or nearly lost one—and understood the need to work harder, to beat back the turn of fate that turned heroes into martyrs.

He cleared branches and cut back trees. He attacked the ditch like a man possessed. When others asked for water, he still didn't stop. He worked until Chief Arnold showed up and ordered him to go home.

"I'm fine," he said, wiping sweat off his forehead.

"You're exhausted."

"No more than you."

"Yes, more than me. Get out of here, Kimball, or

I'll have you dragged out. I don't need any more people in the hospital."

"Yes, sir."

He spun on his heel and left, driving to Josh's apartment, where he changed and showered. With effort, he managed to ignore the eerie silence of the place and tried not to compare it to the day they'd cleaned out Tommy's apartment with his grieving parents.

When he arrived at the hospital, he had lasagna and bread sticks from their favorite Italian place concealed in a bag beneath his coat. The floor nurse gave him a suspicious glare—no doubt from the smell of garlic and tomatoes—but, since his name was on the list of approved visitors, let him pass.

He slipped inside the room to the sight of Josh pushing lime Jell-O around on his dinner plate.

"I'm about to make your day, pal."

Josh grinned. "Thank God. Somebody normal who doesn't want to poke, prod or stick me. And when did floor nurses get so ancient and mean? I remember those cardiac-rehab nurses we dated…" He sighed.

Steve pulled out the bag and set it on the tray hovering over Josh's lap. Except for the bandage across his shoulder and the hospital gown, his buddy looked good. "What do you smell?"

"Antiseptic, overboiled chicken and—" He broke off as his eyes lit. "Lasagna and bread sticks from Cardosa's." He seized the bag, pulling out the foil-covered trays. "Oh, God. Maybe I did die."

Steve flinched at the reminder of how close another friend had come to death.

"Stop already," Josh said, punching him lightly in the stomach. "It'll take more than a tree branch to take me down."

Steve popped open the lid of the bread stick container. "Looks like it took you down pretty good."

"Yeah." Josh rubbed his chest. "I'm gonna hurt like hell tomorrow. Don't suppose you brought a beer?"

"You'll have to settle for a morphine drip."

Shrugging, Josh dug into the meal.

They talked about everything except the stuff Steve knew he had to address. Baseball, NASCAR, the upcoming college football season. The casual rhythm they fell into made it even harder to broach a serious subject.

"Where's Laine?" Josh asked as Steve tossed the empty cartons back in the bag.

"Home, I guess."

"You *guess*? What the hell happened there? How long was I out?"

Now's as good a time as any.

"We've got some issues to work out, but—"

"Issues to work out?" Josh flopped back onto his pillows. "Are you crazy, man? She's nuts about you. You're nuts about her. Live happily ever after. Make me a godfather. And have some boys, while you're at it. I'm really good at PlayStation football—"

"I didn't give up the jumping because of what the doctor said. I gave it up because I lost my edge. I couldn't deal with it anymore."

The confession came out in a rush, like a wound that had to turn red and ugly before healing.

"I know," Josh said.

Steve stared at him. "What do you mean, *you know?*"

"I've known you a long time, man. I could see the look in your eyes. The fire was gone."

"I didn't want to come back."

"You did it for Tommy. There's no shame in it, Steve. That's what they trained us to do. Recognize when you gotta give it up."

Steve looked at his friend of so many years. They'd shared apartments, fought against the worst of fires, laughed through troubles with women and friends. Together. There was no judgment in his eyes. And he felt lousy that he'd even considered the idea.

"Hell, I'm thinking that tree was trying to send me a message today."

A smile tugged at Steve. "*You* retire?"

"Yeah. Maybe. I see you and Laine together. Maybe I could find something like that."

Steve sank onto the side of the bed. "Just don't screw it up when you do."

Laine had offered him everything he'd ever wanted.

And instead of holding on to her, he'd run in the other direction—again.

LAINE SAT on the sun-porch swing, rocking back and forth and staring at the darkening sky. Flashes of lightning flickered in the distance. Ash and the smell of smoke permeated the air.

Rain could mean the end. Of the fire. Of the fear and uncertainty. Her time in California. Her time with Steve.

She wanted it. Dreaded it.

She'd found so much on this trip—a new sense of what she could accomplish professionally. How far she could push herself and get the shots her job required. The realization that maybe her sister could manage just fine on her own. A renewal of her friendship with Denise. A new friend in Cara. A new connection with her aunt.

She wanted to find joy in those things. But her worries about Steve smothered everything.

She heard footsteps behind her. "Smells like rain," Aunt Jen said.

Laine didn't have the strength to argue with her about packing anymore. She understood her need to *hope* everything would work out, but she didn't understand her absolute *belief* in it.

"If you lose the house and want to leave town for a while, you can come stay with me," Laine said.

"I'm not losing the house."

"You will leave with me in the morning, though, right?"

"I brought you something." Aunt Jen rounded the swing, handed her a full glass of wine, then sat beside her with her own glass.

As far as Laine knew, Aunt Jen's drinking was pretty much limited to Christmas and her cousin Susie's wedding, when Jen and her friends had drunk too much champagne, taken over the karaoke machine and bellowed Dean Martin songs the rest of the night.

She might not show it, but the stress was obviously getting to her. "We'll rebuild," she said quickly, not knowing what the devil she'd do if Jen broke down now. "I'll help you, you know that, don't you?"

Jen cast her an irritated look. "We won't need to rebuild. Always the pessimist. You didn't get that from my genes."

"Somebody has to be practical. Somebody has to think ahead."

"Maybe so, but the pictures I saw weren't taken by a pessimist."

Laine clenched the stem of her glass. "What pictures?"

"The ones underneath your purse on the hall table."

"You went through my stuff?"

"How else am I supposed to know what's going on?" She sipped her wine. "Is that why you're sad? Because Steve is jumping out of helicopters?"

Laine didn't bother to ask how her aunt knew she was upset. "No, that's not why I'm sad."

"Well, spill it, missy," she said when Laine didn't elaborate. "I'm not getting any younger."

Vividly recalling the weight and length of Aunt Jen's crowbar, Laine wasn't about to go into too much detail. "Steve feels guilty about Josh getting hurt. And about Tommy dying." There was a great deal more to it than that, of course, but those two events had triggered his uncertainty and confusion.

Aunt Jen huffed. "*Men.* They think the world revolves around them. And what's that got to do with you anyway?"

"I asked him to come back to Texas with me when this is all over. He ran in the other direction."

"I'm gettin' my crowbar."

Laine laid her hand on her arm. "Let's not."

"Just so you know it's there."

"He's not trying to hurt me. He thinks—" She stopped for a moment, considering. "He thinks he betrayed his friends by retiring as a smoke jumper. He thinks he's not—"

"Not what?"

What occurred to her sounded stupid, and kind of dramatic, but Laine was fairly certain it was true. "He thinks he's not heroic enough."

"And you do?"

"Yes."

"Sounds like he's the one with the problem."

"But I love him." She stared at her hands. "So it's my problem, too."

Surprisingly, Jen didn't say anything further. She just laid her arm across Laine's shoulders and hugged her tight. They sat that way, pushing the swing back and forth until the phone rang.

Aunt Jen got up to answer it, then came back with the cordless receiver and held it out to her. "It's Steve."

Laine swallowed her dread and took the receiver. "Hi."

"Hi," he said, sounding distant. "Are you and Aunt Jen packed?"

Actually, she thought it was unlikely her aunt would leave even if the Axminster rug started smoking beneath her feet. "As much as we can be," she said to Steve, who certainly had plenty on his own mind.

"Good." He cleared his throat. "I'm not going to come by tonight. I'm exhausted, but I'll see you tomorrow, okay?"

Laine waited for anger to slide over her. He was being a jerk. Stubborn and unreasonable. But nothing cut into her misery. "Okay," she found herself saying.

"Good night, Laine."

She hung up the phone and rose from the swing. "I'm going to bed. I've had it."

Aunt Jen stared up at her. "You're pale."

"Because I'm tired." She leaned over and kissed her aunt's forehead. "You should get some rest, too. We're supposed to be out by seven."

"I'm going to stay up and watch the storm."

Shaking her head, Laine trudged up the stairs. In her room, she sank onto the bed. The bed where Steve had once lain as he teased and seduced her.

Flopping back, she pulled her pillow over her face so Aunt Jen wouldn't hear and cried.

She and Steve had broken up before because he wanted to be a smoke jumper. Now they might break up because he didn't.

Somewhere, Cupid was laughing his naked ass off.

11

THEY WOKE TO dark clouds and wind.

Even though Aunt Jen's divine rain seemed imminent, as the first spurt of coffee poured into the pot, the fire department sirens and warnings were echoing through the streets.

Aunt Jen looked as if she'd stayed awake all night, but she stood in the center of the kitchen with a single suitcase and a determined expression on her softly lined face. The storm might not arrive in time to save her precious home, and Laine had no idea how to comfort her.

She poured their coffee into plastic mugs, then gathered her overnight bag, and they headed outside. Ash covered the ground and swirled through the air. She coughed as smoke invaded her lungs. They wouldn't last long out here without masks. In the yard next door, Denise and her parents were taking pictures in front of their house. The sight brought angry tears to Laine's eyes.

As she loaded the bags in her car, she considered suggesting the same thing for her aunt, but she didn't have the strength to go another round with her, and figured her camera was probably better served pointed in another, less personal direction. No matter how this affected her family, she still had a job to do.

She started to toss her purse onto the passenger seat of her rental car, but Aunt Jen caught her arm and snagged the pictures peeking from the top of the bag.

"Show them to him," she said, shoving the photos beneath her nose. "Make him understand this is how you see him. Any man who'd turn away from that doesn't deserve your love." Then she spun on her sensible heels and stomped off to her own car.

Laine stared from her to the pictures. The one of just Cara's arm and the blue sky, the progression of Steve hoisting himself into the chopper, then the final one where he stood, exhausted and frustrated, just inside the door. His instincts to protect, to right at least some of the world's wrongs—just another thing she loved about him.

Wait a minute. Her gaze jumped to her aunt. Had Jen stayed up all night not thinking about her house but trying to figure out how to fix her and Steve's relationship?

The woman was either crazy or a saint.

She'd just started after her when she heard the loud roar of a diesel engine. She turned as the bright red fire engine drew even with the driveway.

Steve, dressed in full gear, including helmet and gas mask, jumped off the back of the slowly moving truck and strode in her direction. When he reached her, the only part of him not obscured by equipment was his blue eyes.

Resentment and frustration over this whole mess finally pushed Laine past her sadness. She'd confessed her love, and he'd frozen, then run in the other direction.

I believe this is take two of "Steve and Laine's Breakup."

She'd feared his rejection from the beginning. Her heart had warned her, and she'd ignored its flare of desperation. So maybe—despite Josh's call late last night, reassuring her that Steve was crazy about her, and despite the successes of her trip—she'd have to live with one big fat failure.

But she wasn't going down without a fight.

Show them to him, Aunt Jen had said.

Could he really find a way to see what she did? Would he understand that getting up after falling down is what makes a hero, not jumping out of planes or fighting fires?

"You need to get going," he said, his voice muffled by the mask.

Oh, I'll show him, all right.

"Don't I look like I'm going?" She pushed the pictures against his chest, then stormed past him.

He followed. "Laine, stop."

She kept moving, walking up to the fire engine. "Hey, Jeff!" When the chief stuck his head out of the passenger window, she asked, "Can I hang out with you guys today?"

He shook his head. "Maybe later. I've got to supervise these évacuations."

"But—"

"It's not safe now, Laine. Later I'll have to go up in the chopper. You can come then."

Truthfully, Laine had taken more pictures of fires than she ever wanted to in her lifetime, but somehow she didn't think her editor would agree. "Fine. Call me on my cell." She stepped back, bumping into Steve. Without turning around, she added, "Be careful."

"Does that go for me, too?" Steve asked.

She turned, staring up at him, noting he'd dropped his helmet and gas mask by his side on the ash-strewn lawn. A lump rose in her throat, which she swallowed. "You know it does."

He waved the stack of pictures. "What's this about?"

She took them and shifted to the close-up of his face after he'd climbed back into the chopper. "What do you see when you look at this picture?"

"Where—"

"I took it the day you chased that photographer through the woods." She handed him back the stack and remained silent while he flipped through them.

The fact that a roaring wildfire was likely to tear through this very spot in a matter of hours didn't concern her at the moment. The knowledge that he'd be fighting that fire while the town held its breath would just have to wait.

"I see my frustration at not being able to catch that guy." He met her gaze. "Why? What do you see?"

"I see your determination to try again."

He glanced at the picture, then at her.

She leaned toward him and kissed his cheek. "That's what a hero does."

She strode back to her car and climbed inside. She backed out of the driveway and onto the street with her heart pounding. As she glanced in the mirror she saw him tuck the pictures inside his jacket.

Maybe…

Once Aunt Jen's car fell in line behind her, she headed down the street and toward the Elks Lodge, where the neighborhood had decided to gather. Laine was surprised Aunt Jen didn't want to go to the church, but the lodge was closer, and the church was pretty full already with the evacuees from a few days ago.

The sky was actually spitting rain as Laine got out of her car in the busy parking lot. She met a smiling Denise at the door. "Looks like Jen's plan worked."

"But maybe not in time," Laine said. "We need more than this."

"She's a pessimist," Aunt Jen said as she walked up. "Doesn't get it from me, I assure you."

Denise slid her arm around Jen's waist. "We're about to start a new round of bridge. Want to be my partner?"

Jen eyed her closely. "Do you cheat?"

"No, of course not."

"Don't worry. I'll teach you."

Smiling for the first time all day, Laine followed them into the large gymnasium, where dozens of tables and chairs had been set up, along with cots, sleeping bags and air mattresses. People milled about, holding coffee cups or cans of soda, chatting in small groups. A few teenage boys were entertaining a mass of toddlers in the far corner, as they played basketball on a tiny plastic goal. A few card games had broken out along the tables.

When Laine had visited seven years earlier, Aunt Jen's neighbors had mostly been widowed women and couples her age, but she knew many of them had sold their high-maintenance homes and new, younger families had moved in. She tried not to think about the prize rose gardens, swing sets and tree houses that dotted the neighborhood being consumed by the hungry flames.

She joined her aunt, her elderly friends, Denise and her parents at a table near the right-side wall. Denise and Jen were smiling at the hands they were dealt. Laine pulled her camera out of her bag and began photographing the people around her. The process of framing the shots, sliding the zoom lens back and forth relaxed her.

No matter what these people lost—even if it was everything—they'd recover. They'd rebuild. Better and stronger. At the moment, even her worries about her aunt's willingness to leave seemed silly and unfounded. Aunt Jen wouldn't risk her life over wood and walls.

"Anybody seen Mildred?" Aunt Jen asked, glancing around the hall.

"No. Come to think of it," Denise's mother said, "I haven't seen her all morning."

Aunt Jen laid down her cards. "I'd better call her."

But no one answered Mildred's home phone or cell. None of Aunt Jen's neighbors had seen her.

Then, just as Laine was really starting to worry, Aunt Jen announced, "We'll just have to go find her."

Laine angled her head. "Find? *We?*"

"Yep." Aunt Jen headed across the room and toward the door.

Desperate, Laine dashed after her, glancing back at Denise for her support.

"Ms. Baker!"

"Aunt Jen!"

They caught up to her at the door. "You can't just go charging over to Mildred's house."

Aunt Jen planted her hands on her hips. "Why not?"

Since the answer to that seemed obvious, Laine glanced at Denise.

"The evacuations," her friend said.

"The roadblock," Laine added.

"The fire," they both said.

Aunt Jen waved her hand and started into the parking lot. "I can get around that."

Laine snagged her by the arm. "I'll call Steve. He'll find Mildred."

"He'll be busy," Aunt Jen said.

"Let's at least try," Laine said as she dialed.

His voice mail immediately picked up; he didn't have the phone on.

She left a message, then dialed Cara's cell phone. There was no answer, and she wondered where Cara was. Maybe she'd suited up and joined the others at the front line. Though she focused on arson these days, she knew Cara had started as a firefighter just like everyone else.

"I'm not going to charge the fire, you know," Aunt Jen said, sounding frustrated. "We can go down the back road and avoid the roadblock. It goes right by Mildred's driveway. If her car's not there, we'll leave."

Laine exchanged a look with Denise and didn't bother to ask what they'd do if her car *was* there. Personally, Laine had had enough excitement to last her quite a while, but it looked as if she was going to have one more adventure.

What if Mildred had fallen down the stairs? What if she was unconscious? Hurt? Or both?

"We'll be back," she said to Denise as she dialed Cara's number again.

"A CAT," STEVE MUTTERED. "I think I've been here before."

"An angry cat, don't forget," Cara said.

They continued to jog down the street toward Mildred Moorehead's house—the distraught owner of the cat in question. Mildred, it seemed, had spent the morning trying to coax her prize Himalayan out from under the bed in the guest room. When it seemed apparent that Snuffles had no plans to evacuate, Mildred had called 911.

Steve ran his hand across his chest, the pictures Laine had given him still tucked beneath his coat. He couldn't exactly explain why he'd left them there. Maybe because they were the only part of her he could hold on to at the moment.

He'd gotten her message loud and clear—quit obsessing about the choices he'd made, about accidents he couldn't change. Realize that what he did—what he'd done—was valuable.

He'd faced Josh about his retirement and his fears. During his mostly sleepless night, he'd even somewhat accepted that his father, a hero if ever there was one, might have done the same thing.

Laine believed in him. Did anything else matter? Not as far as he was concerned. Now, if he could only undo the moment he'd walked away from her yesterday, everything would be perfect.

And, by the way, wouldn't it be nice if this damn rain would get on with it and save Aunt Jen's neighborhood?

The storm hovered just on the edge of the area, the rain splattering against the asphalt in big, widely scattered drops. Not enough to make a difference. He had to do better with Laine. He had to overwhelm and barrage her with the love he felt for her. She probably wouldn't forgive him quickly or easily— and he hardly blamed her—but he was ready for the challenge. The most important challenge of his life.

When they rounded the corner, he noticed Mildred-the-Hysterical-Neighbor's front door was wide open, smoke streaming out, and the lady herself was standing in the yard. A familiar car was parked, headlights out, in the driveway.

"What the hell?" Cara asked, obviously noticing the same thing. "Who—"

She didn't say anything else as they broke into a sprint. The wind gusted across them, blowing ash and leaves in their path. Steve was trying to figure out how Aunt Jen had gotten past the roadblock, when he realized which house he was looking at.

This particular driveway didn't end at the house. It continued through the backyard.

He knew, from the drawings he'd seen that morning, that the driveway connected to the main road behind the neighborhood. They hadn't left a guard there because the small group of neighbors who had access to it had assured them it was gated and locked.

Obviously, Aunt Jen knew the combination.

As they reached the front yard, a brisk wind gust swirled around them, and the roof burst into flames.

Mildred screamed. "Hurry, hurry!" she shouted, frantically waving her hand. "They came to get me, and I told them about Snuffles. I told them you were coming, but they went in after her anyway, then the smoke started—"

"They?" Cara asked.

"Jen Baker and her niece, Laine."

"Ah, hell," Cara said.

While she called in the report to the chief, Steve darted through the front door, calling Laine's name.

The house was filled with smoke. An ember from the main fire had probably landed near the house, smoldering for hours in the walls, then bursting with the need for more fuel and oxygen.

With his mask and tank of air, he could survive comfortably for a while. Laine and Jen didn't have that option.

His pulse pounding in his temples and calling her name again, he darted up the stairs. He could hear Cara's communications to the chief through the receivers in his ears, but he blocked it out and prayed for a sound from inside the house.

Nothing.

As the smoke thickened and fire crackled, his thoughts went to his father, as they had many times in the past when he'd run into a burning building. His dad had saved two civilians and a rookie firefighter before the flaming warehouse's ceiling had collapsed unexpectedly and claimed his life. That was the standard heroes were judged by in his town, in his family. He could never equal his father's sacrifice. Didn't want to.

He'd given up smoke jumping because he'd realized he was recklessly sacrificing himself, and, in the process, his team. Josh and Laine were right. Retiring was the smart thing to do. Maybe even the heroic thing to do.

Hollering for Laine again, he raced down the hall to the right.

And nearly ran over her.

"Ow!"

Dropping to his knees, he found himself nose to gas mask with her. He blurted out the first thing that came to his mind. "I love you."

Through the mask he wound up sounding more like Darth Vader than a romantic lover.

Eyes wide, she leaned toward him. "I—" She coughed.

"Not now, boy," Aunt Jen said as she crawled up behind Laine. "We're in mortal danger here."

Steve stroked Laine's cheek with his gloved hand. "Later, then?"

She nodded, adjusting her hold on the fluffy black-and-white cat tucked beneath her arm.

"I got 'em, Cara," he said into his communications mic. "Upstairs hall, to the right."

As he slid his arm around Aunt Jen's waist, Cara arrived to help Laine down the stairs. They rushed out the front door, and other firefighters moved in with hoses and axes. Two paramedics with stretchers met Steve at the curb. He scooped Aunt Jen off her feet, then set her down on the gurney. The paramedics checked her vitals and placed an oxygen mask over her face, while she glared at him in annoyed silence.

Confident they could best help Jen at the moment, Steve patted her blue-veined hand, pulled off his own mask, then turned to find Laine.

The moment she handed off the cat to a grateful and crying Mildred, Laine tried to lurch past him toward the stretcher.

He caught her by the waist. "She'll be fine. Let them work."

Coughing, Laine pulled out of his hold.

"What were the two of you thinking, running into that house after a cat?" he asked.

The cat in question, now comfortable in Mildred's arms, stared at him with its eerily pale blue eyes.

"Aunt Jen realized Mildred was missing, so we used the back entrance to check on her. When we got here, Mildred was hysterical over the cat. She couldn't reach her, and she's not small enough to crawl under the bed."

"So petite and spry Aunt Jen graciously offered to get her."

"Naturally."

"Why didn't you call 911?"

Laine cast an annoyed glance at her aunt. "Call for help? Now, why didn't I think of that?" When she looked back at him, she added, "I knew all of you were here. I kept trying your cell. And we didn't realize the house was on fire until we got upstairs and found it filled with smoke."

"She needs oxygen, Steve," Chief Arnold said, appearing next to them and drawing Laine to another stretcher.

Laine dug in her heels. "I don't. I'm fine."

Chief Arnold ignored her protests and lifted her onto the stretcher. "Just sit. You'll feel better."

A paramedic placed a mask over her nose and mouth, then wrapped a blood pressure cuff around her arm. Steve noticed she didn't pull away from either man's touch, the way she had his.

"No need to fight, kids," the paramedic said. "I thought you were in love."

His partner nudged him, and they laughed.

Of course Cara picked that moment to walk up. She stood next to the chief. They both exchanged a look of pity.

Why couldn't he have waited? Over dinner and candlelight? The rose petals had been a nice touch before.

Instead, he'd embarrassed himself quite nicely by blurting out his feelings over the radio during a major disaster operation for half of northern California to hear.

But then, waiting for the right time wasn't an option anymore either.

He stood in front of Laine and wished he could do this somewhere else. *Anywhere* else. When she looked up at him, he said, "I love her, but I'm not sure what she thinks. I've been a real jerk."

Pulling off her mask, she pursed her lips. "Well...you were a jerk. And stubborn. And—"

"Good grief, girl," Aunt Jen said after tossing off her own mask. "It's not as bad as all that."

"I'm getting there." She laid her palm against his cheek. "But I love you anyway."

As the guys cheered, Steve pulled her into his arms and kissed her, relief and happiness flooding his heart. He knew he would always be a hero to her, so no one else mattered. Silently, as he held her tight against him, he swore she would never regret taking a chance on him, on their love for each other.

Unbelievably, at that moment, it started to rain. Really rain. A steady curtain of pouring rain that soaked him and Laine from head to toe in seconds.

She closed her eyes and tipped her head back. The cheers and claps by everyone around him doubled in volume. Aunt Jen simply nodded in satisfaction.

Snuffles was probably the only creature within ten miles who wasn't happy.

Laine took the cat from Mildred, then walked around the back of the ambulance to tuck her inside. Steve followed her and took the opportunity of a bare minimum of privacy to trap her against the doors. "I'm sorry I made us so public," he said.

She ran her hands down the front of his jacket, gripping the lapels, which were slick with rain. "I thought it was quite heroic of you."

"Ah, yes. Heroic." He grinned. "Thanks for the pictures."

"And what did you learn?"

He smoothed her sopping hair off her face. "I learned I should see myself through your eyes. That giving up smoke jumping was not a failure but a success."

"That's a pretty good start. You and Josh must have had some talk yesterday."

"Josh?"

"He called me late last night and told me not to give up on you."

"Did he?" He made a mental note to thank his friend, then recalled the panic that overwhelmed him when she'd walked away from him. "I thought I'd blown it. Again."

Blinking the rain out of her eyes, she looped her arms around his neck. "I'm a bit more determined than I was before. The pictures, by the way, were Aunt Jen's idea."

"Does this mean we have to name our first child Jen?"

She raised her eyebrows. "From *I love you* to children all in one morning?"

"Oh, yeah." Figuring this was as good a mood as he was likely to ever find her in, Steve snagged her hand and dropped to one knee.

12

A LOT HAD HAPPENED in a week, Laine decided. The steady rain over Fairfax had lasted three full days, drenching the wildfire and the ground. During that time, she and Steve had moved into a motel on the edge of town. They'd talked, laughed, made love and made plans for a wedding. Steve had wanted to elope, but Laine wanted her friends and family around her, so they compromised with a quickie wedding on Saturday in Georgia.

Steve had shared his desire to become an arson investigator, and Laine had given her unwavering support. They'd spent an afternoon picking out rings at Fairfax Jewelry. They'd shared a celebration toast of their engagement at Suds—and Laine had taken down the chief in a game of eight-ball that would no doubt become legendary.

Though the fire had ultimately claimed ten homes in the Arbor Acres neighborhood, Aunt Jen's street was mostly untouched, and the firefighters had saved Mildred's house. Unfortunately, the final total of forestland acres burned was over ten thousand. And photographer Newton Granger had been arraigned in federal court after Cara and Chief Arnold determined the hot-spot fire likely had been started by his campfire.

When she arrived in Georgia on Thursday, she broke the news to her sister.

"I did something wild," she blurted the moment Cat answered the phone.

"You?" The surprise in Cat's voice was obvious.

"I got engaged."

"To who?"

"That guy I dated years ago, when I lived with Aunt Jen for the summer. His name is Steve. Wanna come to a wedding on Saturday?"

After a long pause, Cat cleared her throat. "I— Sure I'll be there. Where else you gonna get a maid of honor?"

"No kidding?"

"No kidding. Maybe I'll even bring a date with me. Someone special."

Sticking to her new vow that everybody should be as deliriously happy as she was, Laine resisted the urge to ask what kind of motorcycle he would arrive on. "Really?"

"Yeah," she admitted softly, though she didn't elaborate, and Laine didn't press. She didn't want to start another argument.

Laine gave her sister all the wedding details, then realized that the short notice would prevent Tess and Grace from attending. Cat promised to get them all together for a last call drink at Temptation, if Laine could come through Kendall early the next week.

"I still can't believe you're doing this," Cat said. "Does Mom know?"

After Laine assured her that their mother was coming, her sister continued, "Okay, I got it. Saturday the twenty-fifth. You can count on me."

Count on Cat? This was going to take some getting used to.

"Maybe we can find a few minutes to talk," Cat said. "A lot's been going on with me, too. I'm thinking about going back to college. I even have all the paperwork filled out."

"Wow." Her sister really *was* getting her life together. "Then the bonus money I earned for the cover of *Century* is going to come in handy."

"You got the cover? Really?"

"Yep." Though Steve turned bright red whenever anybody mentioned he was going to be famous once the magazine came out. "And it's definitely enough for tuition."

"You keep the money. Start a college fund for your first baby. Oh, God, you're not pregnant, are you?"

Laine laughed. "Definitely not."

"Okay, because one bit of wild, impulsive Laine news per day is my quota," Cat said. "As for the money, I mean it, I'll be fine. I think the two of us are going to come out a little better than we expected on the furniture and fixture sales."

Cat's generosity reminded Laine that her sister had been handling the closing of Temptation like a pro. Her accomplishments made Laine feel doubly guilty for bailing out on her. Her voice soft, she said, "You've been amazing the last couple of weeks, you know. I felt so overwhelmed when I left, as if everyone was relying on me to fix everything."

"If you'd wanted out, all you had to do was say so," Cat said stiffly.

"No, I couldn't. Temptation meant too much to you and Mom. And don't worry about the closing. I'll be back to help."

"Seriously, you don't need to. I've got everything under control."

The rushed tone of her sister's voice raised Laine's suspicions about whether everything was really fine, but Cat had done so much on her own, Laine had no intention of letting her think she didn't trust her. It was about time somebody relied on Cat for more than just a cold beer.

"I'm here if you need me," she said to Cat.

"I know you are. You always have been. I'll see you Saturday."

When they signed off, Laine felt better about her relationship with her sister than she had in years. And knowing that Cat could take care of herself, Laine took a chance careerwise, too. She called her editor to see if she could work on a freelance basis from her new home in Georgia. Mac was so pleased with her pictorial on the wildfire, he agreed.

Over the next few days, she met Steve's older brother, Ben, and his outrageous wife, Monica, who suggested Laine wear a really short white miniskirt for the ceremony—which she politely refused. She'd instead chosen a simple white strapless dress of lace and satin.

She met his sister, Skyler, who was several months pregnant with her first child, and her husband, Jack, who gave her a box of lingerie as a wedding present that made her jaw drop. Even Chief Arnold sent a gift—a CD recording of the on-scene dialogue where Steve had first confessed his love.

On Saturday, all the Kimballs, plus her mom, Denise, Aunt Jen, Josh and Cat stood around her as the mayor of Baxter began the ceremony.

"I never anticipated I'd be married by an Elvis impersonator," Laine said as she glanced around City Hall. "At least not outside of Vegas."

"It's getting to be a tradition in our family," her groom said, squeezing her hand.

"We call to order this sacred ritual of hunka, hunka burnin' love."

"Mayor, please," Ben said, closing his eyes.

"All right, all right." The portly mayor—clad in a white rhinestone-studded jumpsuit, cape, gold sunglasses and large belt buckle—waved his hand. "Maybe the more traditional version."

"Please," Ben said with a wink in her direction.

She smiled her thanks, the mayor flipped through his notes, then continued by saying, "We are gathered here today…"

Truthfully, Laine made it through the ceremony and reception only because she knew Steve was the reward at the end. She longed for his arms, the sound of his voice, the love she knew she'd see in his eyes.

"Having fun?" he said, embracing her from behind.

"I am now." She leaned back against his chest, letting the heat from his body seep into hers, inhaling his familiar scent. She'd stepped outside their bubble of contentment for the wedding, but she wanted to get back there as soon as possible. They had seven years to make up for. "Any chance we can blow this party?"

He kissed the side of her neck. "I'm so glad you asked." Sliding his hand into hers, he led them around the edge of the room, behind the cake they'd already cut, Steve snagging a bottle of champagne on the way. As they darted down a back hall, Josh was pulling Aunt Jen onto the dance floor, and Cat had taken over the bar.

They climbed inside his SUV and headed home. They'd decided to spend their first night as man and wife in his lake house, the home they'd share together.

He parked in the garage, but insisted on going around to the front door, so he could carry her over the threshold. "Something about this wedding should be traditional," he said as he swept her into his arms.

"We got married." She slid her fingers through the hair at his temple. "That's enough for me." As he laid her on his king-size bed, amid scattered rose petals, she added, "We got some nice gifts."

He trailed kisses down her throat. "Really?"

"I particularly like the one from your sister."

He paused. "It's sort of legendary that my sister sells very racy lingerie out of the back room of her dress shop."

"She does indeed."

"That sounds like a good gift."

"I think you'll like it."

He cupped her breast. "Later, though."

They made love in their bed, with candlelight flickering off their skin, with sighs and promises of love whispered in the night.

Later, as she lay with her head against his chest and he stroked her hair, she said quietly, "I got you a present."

"I got you one, too."

She lifted her head. "You did?"

He grinned. "A week on a resort in Mexico. We leave tomorrow."

More paradise? Going back to the real world was going to be a jarring experience. "As long as we swing through Kendall first. My sister is throwing a last call party. And I need to pick up my bikini from my apartment."

He slid his finger along her bare shoulder. "I don't think you'll need it."

"Probably not." She reached over him and under the bed, pulling out a gold-wrapped package. "My gift's not quite that elaborate."

He lifted himself to a seated position and turned on the bedside light. After he tore open the package and the picture of him, Josh and Tommy was revealed, his gaze jumped to hers.

"It's one I took years ago. I thought you might like it. In a way, he got us back together."

He cupped the back of her head and pulled her close. "It's perfect. He'd be happy for us."

"I love you. Be my hero forever?"

"Gladly. That's a job I'm keeping forever."

The
Temptation
Years
1984–2005

<u>Autographs</u>

Temptation—
Thanks for the memories.
Barbara Daly

Temptation is and always
will be home. The line
and its readers gave me
my start. I love you all!
Carly Phillips

Temptation always had the heroines I
wanted to be – and the heroes I wanted
to have!
Cindi Myers

Thanks for the memories,
Temptation! And thanks
especially for putting me
in touch with so many
wonderful readers. I'll miss you.
Cara Summers

I ♡ Temptations!
I made my Harlequin
debut there & found
some of my 'fave
authors between
Temptation covers.
Temptresses RULE! ☺
Dawn Atkins

I'll miss our steamy
nights and laughs, always!
Julie McBride

My dear Temptation,
What can I say? You've
given me some wonderful reads,
launched my career, and introduced
me to a whole slew of new friends.
You had a fabulous run and I'll miss you!
Love –
Julie Kenner

Dear Temptation,
Thanks for giving this
"nice girl" a chance to be
"just a little bit naughty."
Darlene Gardner

It is with great sadness I say goodbye
to Temptation. So many wonderful
stories... So many great authors. Thanks
to editors Brenda Chin and Jennifer Green
for giving me a home, and to the
Temptresses for making me feel so
welcome!

All my best,

Jill Monroe

Dear Temptation,
You were the first Harlequin line
I fell in love with as a reader,
and the line I felt honored
to break into as an author.
Colleen Collins

Thanks for my ten tempting years!
Heather MacAllister
June 1995 – June 2005

For all the friends I've made and stories I've loved-- It was my pleasure to be led into Temptation

Jacquie D'Alessandro

Thanks for giving me my start! I'll always be a "Temptation" writer.

Kate Hoffmann

Dear Temptation-

What a run! As a reader, I learned anything is possible if you approach life with a little sass.

Heck, I learned the same as a writer.

Here's to sass!

Julie Elizabeth Leto

"Temptation" was right there at the start of SEXY and HOT. She'll be remembered with love and a quickened pulse by

Barbara Delinsky

My love and undying gratitude to my readers. I couldn't have enjoyed seventeen fabulous years at Temptation without you!

Kristine Rolofson

Temptation will always
have a home on my bookshelf!
KRISTIN GABRIEL

First Kiss. First lover. First book.
I'll never forget the Temptation!
Smooches,
Cheryl

My keeper shelf is stuffed
full of Temptation stories
and I've loved every month
of this awesome line! Thanks
for all the great reading :)
Jane Rock

Writing for the Temptation line
helped me to find my voice as
a writer... I'm proud to be
forever linked to this line as
a Temptress! Stephanie Bond

Happy retirement,
Temptation!
You've brought me so
much joy and laughter
through the years. It's
hard to watch you go.
— Wendy Etherington

For years, Temptations were the books I loved to read. Becoming a Temptress was a dream come true and forged lasting friendships with both authors and Readers. Thank you, Temptation, for the fun, laughter, and good times!

Janelle Denison

Not only did Temptation give me my start, it also gave me some of the greatest friends of my life. I'll always be honored to have been a Temptress!

Leslie Kelly

Thanks to Harlequin — You let your writers spread their wings and fly. We're touched the sky.

Sandra Chastain

Thank you, Temptation, for giving me special friends I'll value for a lifetime. The camaraderie and talent within the line, and the readers who gave it popularity, made writing for Temptation a very special time in my life. I'll miss the fun more than I can say.

Lori Foster

My very first book was a Temptation, so the line will always hold a special place in my heart

I wish all the talented authors, brilliant editors and, most of all, the faithful readers all the best for the future.

Always a Temptress!
Nancy Warren

From getting that first call for CALL ME on national televisio to being a part of the line's 15th Anniversary... thanks, Temptation, I for all of the memories! Alison Kent

There is nothing like diving into a phat, totally fun story — I have only the best memories of writing for Temptation.
Carla Neggers

Temptation Romances taught me to believe. Not only in the power of love, but also in the power of being a woman. & being published in the line was the ultimate expression of all the things I learned from the line, independence, belief in myself, and faith that success on every level was within my grasp. Thank you HQ for giving women strong, sexy role models to show them the way!

Mara Fox

Hey, sweet Temptation! What a kick
hanging out with you. Thanks for the
memories! XXOO Vicki Lewis Thompson

True love stories never
have endings —
Friends 4-ever!
Lori & Tony
aka
Toni Collins

JoAnn Ross

I can resist everything
but Temptations!!
Kathleen
O'Reilly

HARLEQUIN® *Blaze*™

Romeo, Texas

Where men are cowboys...
and women are determined to catch them!

Meet Josh and Mason McGraw,
Long, lean and legendary.
No women could resist them,
no woman could hold them...until now!

Don't miss seeing the baddest cowboys
in town meet their match in

Kimberly Raye's

latest miniseries

#191 TEXAS FEVER
July 2005

#198 TEXAS FIRE
August 2005

Everything is hotter in Texas!